GIDEON BEAN

AURA & EMBERS BOOK 1

GWEN DEMARCO

CHAPTER 1

Gideon wiped the perspiration from his brow as he trudged across the crematorium's scorching hot parking lot. The sweltering heat from the day still rose from the asphalt in distorted ripples, even though the sun had dipped below the horizon. The walk from his car to the front door was a short distance, but his clothes were already sticking to his skin halfway there. He hadn't met a deodorant yet that could battle the Sunshine State's humidity.

The salty kiss of the ocean breeze gently caressed his face, offering a fleeting moment of relief from the oppressive heat that suffocated the muggy air.

The crematorium building was a one-story squat structure highlighted against the twilight sky by the last rays of sunlight. It was a wide building made of hurricane-proof cement blocks. Someone, in an attempt to give the place a facelift, had taken the liberty to cover the sturdy blocks with fake brick overlays and adorned them further with cheap plastic siding and matching shutters, but had only bothered with the front of the building, leaving the rest as plain cinderblocks covered in tan paint. These additions were clearly an attempt at sophistication, kindling an illusion of a dignified final resting place. To get inside the building, visitors had to climb a few steps onto a diminutive front veranda which was hemmed in by imposing white columns that looked oversized. When Gideon was first hired at the crematorium, he was required to enter through the back door. But the heat, rain, and humidity had made the wooden back door swell and warp. Consequently, Gideon had to enter through the front until Mr. Peterson replaced it. But it'd been nearly a year now, and Gideon didn't expect it to be fixed anytime soon.

Gideon could already hear the distant hum of the ovens. The single still-functioning streetlight hanging overhead showed only one other vehicle in the parking lot besides his small crappy hatchback. The ancient truck was more rust than blue paint, with its gun rack in the back window. Its presence made Gideon huff out a resigned breath.

Gideon's fervent hope that Linus had already left for the day was dashed at the sight of the truck. Linus was a man who only regarded football, guns, and women who were clearly out of his league as worthy subjects of conversation. Gideon was thoroughly sick of those topics, but escaping any conversation was not a luxury granted to him by his coworker. Linus didn't talk *with* Gideon so much as talk *at* him. Gideon let out a slow breath, mentally preparing himself for the unending barrage of talk.

He opened the crematorium's front door and paused in the opening, letting the cool air from inside the building wash over him. The air conditioning was a welcome reprieve from the suffocating humidity of the town of Gulf Breeze. He walked past the lobby, where a viewing room was off to the left, and the main office was to the right. Heading through the door to the back half of the building, he punched the time clock, signaling the beginning of another long night of work. Glancing at the schedule board, he noted the long list of people who awaited their final journey into an oven. Linus stepped around the corner as if on cue. Gideon watched as the heavyset man ambled over with a perpetual layer of sweat ringing his armpits, peeling thick leather gloves off his hands. Gideon ducked his head, hoping that for once Linus would take the hint and not stop for a conversation.

"Hey, Giddy," Linus grunted, mopping his brow with a damp, stained handkerchief.

"Don't call me that," Gideon responded automatically.

"Pssh, whatever. No need to be so uptight, *Giddy*." When Gideon didn't rise to the bait, Linus shrugged. "We got a real load tonight. You're gonna need to fire up all three ovens. Plenty of bodies to burn, thanks to the heat wave taking its toll on the retired snowbirds."

Gideon raised an eyebrow, weary and resigned. It seemed the relentless Florida heat had claimed its usual harvest. He knew all too well the consequences of the southern environment on the weak and elderly. During the hottest months of the year, it sometimes felt like an endless procession of bodies that found their way to his doorstep.

Despite his disheveled appearance, Linus wore a toothy grin; his straight white teeth seemed at odds with the rest of his slovenly air.

"Hey," Linus exclaimed gleefully, dropping his meaty hand to squeeze Gideon's bicep through his sleeve. "Looks like hauling all these bodies around is paying off. I thought you were just a beanpole, but you got some muscles under there."

Gideon shrugged off Linus's touch, keeping the look of distaste off his face. "Gotta go. You know how the boss gets if we get backlogged. Make sure you lock up on your way out."

With those words, Gideon sidled past Linus and escaped to the furnace room to check the ovens. If Linus responded, Gideon didn't hear. He inserted his earbuds, selecting a playlist filled with indie rock and drowning out both Linus and the hum of the ovens.

The weight of the night settled upon his shoulders, quiet and alone, just as he preferred it. Checking over the ovens, Gideon glanced inside each brick-lined cavern, the lingering heat slapping him in the face. Checking the gauges, he watched as the flames leaped and flickered, and he braced himself for the long hours of solitude. He had long since gotten over the spookiness of working the graveyard shift at the crematorium. His imagination no longer conjured a symphony of ghostly whispers and ghastly screams and scratching from inside the incinerators. The occasional moan from the ancient air conditioning unit didn't send his heart galloping any more.

During his first week at the job, he jumped at every little noise. Now the crematorium was no spookier than his day job at the tacky tourist trap, with its shelves stacked with seashell 'art', cheap t-shirts, and rainbow-colored beach umbrellas that usually broke after the first use. Gideon found the tourists scarier than the corpses surrounding him. Not once had anyone in the crematorium yelled at him over an overpriced trinket. It was almost a daily occurrence at Sheryl's Shell Shack.

Gideon turned off most of the lights in the facility, preferring to work in dim lighting. The ovens stood ready, hungry for their macabre feast, and Gideon was their keeper, orchestrating the symphony of fire that would consume the remnants of the town's expired residents.

Humming along to a familiar song, Gideon approached the towering refrigeration unit, his boots echoing through the hall. Stepping inside, its chilled breath sent a shiver down his spine. Three cardboard boxes sat waiting, each on their own gurney. Inside each box would be a corpse awaiting the fiery depths of the retort incinerator. He wheeled the first gurney towards the furnace. The hydraulic hiss punctuated the silence as he raised the stainless-steel platform to be level with the opening in the oven, loud enough to be heard over his music.

Dry heat enveloped him as he neared the oven, its fiery tendrils licking at his sweat-drenched skin. Gideon's elbow-length leather gloves, worn and thick, shielded his hands from the scorching touch of the metal doors. Yet he could feel the residual heat seep into his fingertips, a reminder of the relentless inferno that awaited within. With meticulous care, he checked the metal tags attached to each cloth-wrapped body, comparing it to the dead person's paperwork, ensuring precision in this gruesome symphony of final farewells. Satisfied, he slid the boxes, one by one, into the awaiting maw.

Gideon fell into the easy rhythm of his work: grab a corpse-filled box, check the metal tag attached to the body against the paperwork, slide the box into the oven, and let it roast. Once the furnace had cooled, he swept the ashes and bone shards into the receptacle below. He then ran a high-intensity magnet over the ashes to remove anything that might damage the cremulator which ground the bones and ashes into a sand-like texture. Once the cremulator finished grinding, Gideon put the ashes into a box to be given to the person's relatives.

In the wee hours, Gideon allowed himself a brief respite, stretching his hands above his head, and twisting his torso, groaning in pleasure when his back gave a series of satisfying cracks. Checking his watch, he decided to get one more set of bodies to burn before taking a break. He'd been flirting with the girl at the deli counter of Publix for the last few weeks. He wasn't sure if it was going anywhere, but it never hurt to take a shot. He'd seen her add a few extra slices of ham to his sub sandwich when he'd stopped at the grocery store on the way to work, so perhaps he was finally making some progress on that front.

Inside the fridge, Gideon checked his paperwork before lifting the lid off the next box, revealing an unexpected sight. Normally, the bodies they received were fully wrapped in cloth and their faces were covered. Whoever had put her in the box had only laid the white cloth over the body, instead of wrapping it like usual. The cloth must've shifted off the woman's face sometime during transportation. He checked at the metal tag attached to the corpse, comparing it to the paperwork clutched in his gloved hand. The death certificate was signed and matched the Cremation Permit form. Gideon then checked that the authorization form was properly filled out. He was extra careful checking to ensure the paperwork was at least correctly filled out. Usually, the only time a person was burned in their clothes was when there was a viewing for the family before the cremation – and that only happened during the day shift. No one was allowed in the facility aside from employees after hours.

He started to put the cardboard lid back on the burn box when he spotted some splatters of dried blood on the woman's forehead. Looking around surreptitiously, even though he knew he was alone, he tugged gently on the cloth laid over the woman, fully exposing her face.

As his eyes scanned her lifeless form, Gideon couldn't help but feel a twinge of surprise and sadness. She was young, probably in her late 20s, a stark contrast to the typical elderly who were sent to the crematorium. Her elfin, heart-shaped face possessed a delicate beauty. She was pretty, even in death, with tanned skin and thick wavy dark hair.

Gideon's eyes caught on the gash across her throat, a ghoulish testament to her violent end. He was shocked at the raw brutality of the woman's demise. The flowery summer dress she'd been wearing was drenched in blood. The bloodied clothing troubled Gideon – shouldn't that have been bagged as evidence or something? The woman had clearly been murdered. Not that he had any idea of police procedure, but it just seemed logical. He was surprised that her death hadn't made the news. Gulf Breeze was a sleepy beach town that very rarely had anything newsworthy happen inside its borders.

Gideon's gaze fixated on her dark hair, realizing that it was matted with blood. His eyes were drawn to her hand, noticing a thick ornate ring on her thumb adorned with a vivid red gemstone. Curiosity compelled him to pick up her hand, his gloved fingers tracing her scraped and bruised knuckles. He realized that under the fresh cuts, her knuckles had older, partially healed scabs and faded scars. At first glance, he'd imagined her as a sorority girl, but the layers of injuries indicated something darker.

Double-checking the paperwork, Gideon found no mention of her jewelry being cremated with her. With a heavy sigh, he made the difficult decision to slip the ring from her finger, placing it gently to the side. It was a small act, a gesture of respect. He'd need to go into the main office and see if she had a box of personal belongings. If she did, he'd add the ring to it. He was sure that someone, a friend or family member, maybe a boyfriend, would be glad to get it back. Gideon noted that the ring finger on her left hand didn't have the usual telltales from a wedding ring – no tan lines, no indent from a metal band. There would be no spouse to mourn her loss.

He checked the name on the death certificate out of curiosity. Holding the document to the dim light, he read out loud, "Candace Menet. Huh, you don't look like a 'Candace'."

He gave her one last look, memorizing her face before closing the box once more. Gideon started rolling the gurney towards the incinerator, puzzling over the young woman. He needed to let his boss, Mr. Peterson, know that the coroner's office was getting lazy and not preparing the bodies properly. Gideon figured it was the least he could do for the dead woman.

Sliding her box into the furnace with only the smallest lingering feeling of regret, Gideon started the burn cycle, then returned to the fridge to start the process with the next body. He tried to shake off the thoughts of the woman, but he couldn't stop seeing her heart-shaped face in his mind and wondering what led to her death.

Gideon started to head to the breakroom but decided to push back his lunch break since his appetite had disappeared. Heading to the back room, he poured one of the containers filled with ashes and bone shards into the cremulator. A strange noise had

Gideon turning off the bone grinding machine, his routine momentarily interrupted by a distinct thump echoing through the crematorium. Pulling out his earbuds, he cocked his head, straining to catch the sound once more. After a pause, it sounded again. Removing his gloves, he headed towards the front door – it wouldn't be the first time that a drunken bereaved person showed up at their door, panicking over the thought of a loved one being set on fire.

His steps stuttered to a stop when he got to the reception area and saw no one out front. The only thing in the parking lot was his old Toyota hatchback. When a series of thumps sounded again from further inside the facility, an unsettling chill crawled down his spine. His curiosity piqued, he turned around, ready to follow the noise to its source, his steps growing quicker and more determined. Maybe someone was knocking on the rarely used back door.

CHAPTER 2

When Gideon realized that the noise was coming from the furnace room, he almost had a heart attack. He sprinted towards the towering machines, hitting the emergency stop with a swift motion. A forgotten pacemaker? Or some other hazardous medical device that could wreak havoc on the incinerator? It was an incredibly dangerous situation that had Gideon's hands shaking uncontrollably. It had happened once before – a corpse had been put into the oven with their pacemaker still inside the body – and it had damaged the machine enough that they'd been down a retort oven for almost three weeks. Linus had complained heartily to Gideon that Mr. Peterson had been a raging jerk the entire time until it was fixed.

Now that he'd turned off the oven and the danger was over, frustration mingled with worry as he realized that if the retort was damaged, Mr. Peterson would blame him, even though the device causing the problem should've been removed by the coroner. Gideon's job description did not include checking the bodies for medical devices and personal effects. Thankfully, he rarely had to interact with the beady-eyed scarecrow of a man. One of the perks of the graveyard shift.

Composing a scathing email of complaint in his head – not only had someone missed the ring on the dead woman's finger, but now something else was amiss with a body – Gideon's thoughts were abruptly interrupted by another heavy thump. He jumped like a spooked cat and stared in horror at the middle oven that contained the woman. For a moment, there was complete silence, broken only by Gideon's wheezing breaths.

But then that single thump was followed by a series of frenzied bangs that echoed within the cavernous room. Gideon hesitated for a moment before approaching the oven. He grabbed the fire extinguisher off the wall and held it at the ready as he swung open the door. In one swift motion, he released a cloud of flame retardant into the ominous depths of the oven, the white foam casting an eerie contrast against the darkness within.

The room fell silent, the flurry of thumps subsiding as the foam settled. Gideon stood there, his chest heaving with exertion, a mix of relief and lingering apprehension coursing through his veins. The enigma of those sounds left him bewildered, but the immediate danger seemed to have dissipated.

With a heavy sigh, he knew that he needed to fetch the magnet and see if he could find the medical appliance causing the problem. Not wanting to leave the oven door open, just in case the device was still unstable, he started to close the furnace door when it was suddenly kicked out of his hands.

Gideon's scream pierced the air as he fell backward, his body scrambling away in sheer terror. From the depths of the incinerator emerged a figure, covered in a layer of dark ash and clumps of white retardant. His eyes widened in disbelief as the form solidified into the shape of a woman – a woman with wings of fire sprouting from her back.

She stood before him, completely naked, her fists propped on her hips as she dispassionately looked around the furnace room. Despite her nudity, Gideon's gaze was trapped by the magnificent wings crafted entirely of flames rising from her back. They spanned an impressive width, stretching outwards, licking the walls of the room. The flickering fire formed a mesmerizing display of colors – fiery reds, brilliant oranges, and golden yellows shimmered and pulsated with an ethereal glow.

As she shifted, the flames rippled with energy, casting a bright, radiant light on their surroundings. Each individual flame seemed alive, reminiscent of molten lava.

The wings of fire seemed to possess a life of their own, casting a glow upon the woman's form. She stood tall and regal, her presence both fierce and captivating. In all his twenty-seven years, Gideon had never been so terrified and mesmerized. When the woman turned her gaze on him, it speared him in place, filling him equally with terror and awe.

"Damn it! Did I die again?" The woman said with an aggravated growl. She looked away from Gideon and glanced around the room, bafflement blooming across her features. "Hold up… Where am I?"

"Get back, demon!" Gideon screamed, making the sign of the cross. He wasn't a religious fellow, despite being raised in the church, but in the face of evil, he would grasp any straw to save himself. "Yay, though I walk through the valley of the shadow of—"

"Whoa, whoa. Slow down, dude." The woman raised her hands in a placating gesture, looking at him like *he* was the crazy one. "Shit, you're gonna give yourself a heart attack."

Gideon's words died on his tongue, and he gulped thickly, attempting to gather his wits as confusion mixed with fear swamped him. The gaping wound across her neck was gone, leaving behind unblemished, intact skin.

She stared at Gideon, one eyebrow raised challengingly. "Seriously, where am I? And where the hell is George?"

"Uh, you're at Peterson Cremation Services. I, um, I don't know anything about anyone named George. Are… are you going to kill me?"

"Shit," the woman growled. She rolled her shoulders, and the wings of fire extinguished, leaving Gideon blinking spots from his vision. "How did I end up here? I should be at Tranquil Haven. Man, George really screwed the pooch this time. I'm going to kill him."

He tried to fixate on the woman's face – he really did – but he felt his eyes slip for a split second to the woman's naked form. Following his gaze, the woman glanced downward. Another exasperated exclamation escaped her lips.

"Damn it! That was my favorite dress."

The woman started to look back up but suddenly froze. Slowly, she raised her left hand and stared at it in horror. "Oh no! No, no, no. My ring. Shit." Whirling on her feet, she scrambled back into the incinerator, cursing and yelling.

Gideon scrambled to his feet. "Ma'am! Don't! It's still hot!" he yelped.

Looking over her shoulder, her irritated gaze bore into him.

"I—I have your ring, miss," Gideon managed to stammer out, his voice trembling. "I put it with your paperwork, um, Candace."

"Oh, man. You're a lifesaver! Thank you," she exclaimed. Backing out of the oven, she started to give him a pleased grin, but the smile slipped from her face and she pinned him with an intensely suspicious stare. This close, Gideon could see that her eyes were a light brown, morphing into a reddish-orange ring that encircled her pupil. It reminded him of a solar eclipse. Suspicion and anger flared in her eyes. "How do you know my name?"

Gideon pointed to the metal tag still attached to her wrist. She rolled her eyes when she spied the tag. "Duh," she said with an amused snort.

"No one calls me Candace. It's Dacey." She paused and gave Gideon a look, her mouth firming into a thin line. "Also, if you ever call me Candy, I will eviscerate you. Got it?" He couldn't tell if she was kidding or not.

He dumbly nodded, erring on the side of caution.

"Well? You said you have my ring," she reminded Gideon. "Also, I need clothes. Do you have a lost and found or something?"

"Um, we have some employee lockers. There might be something in one of those."

"That'll do." She stared at Gideon while he, still feeling overwhelmed and stupefied, stared back. Finally, she drew a deep, slow breath, like she was reaching for patience. "Okay, whatever-your-name-is, can you show me where the lockers are located?" Dacey spoke as if talking to a confused and lost toddler.

Gideon jolted, shaking his head at himself. "Sorry, yeah. Follow me. Oh, and um, my name is Gideon."

On the way to the lockers, Gideon stopped at his workstation and gave Dacey her ring back. She slid it back on her thumb with obvious relief.

"I appreciate you saving this for me," Dacey said, giving Gideon a small smile. Until that moment, all her expressions had been etched with shock, annoyance, or confusion. He found himself momentarily captivated by the transformation that unfolded before him. She had the kind of beauty that men wrote sonnets about. His heartbeat started to gallop, and his hands turned clammy. He'd thought she might be a demon, but now that her features weren't marred by a frown, he thought she might be an angel. Gideon could feel the admiring look come over his face but was powerless to stop it. Dacey must've noticed it because the smile instantly dropped from her lips, and she stepped back. Gideon felt like a creep, getting caught smiling like a simpering fool at a naked, vulnerable woman.

She turned away from him and sidled away, putting space between them. Gideon felt like an inept moron. He had no game. Shit, he had *negative* game. There was no way a woman like Dacey would give a loser like him the time of day, and he needed to learn this lesson for good. His ego couldn't take another flop in the romance department.

Gideon showed her the breakroom with its few lockers. Looking over the stand of lockers, she then turned and gave Gideon's outfit a once over. "You're not too much bigger than me. Do you have any spare clothes here?"

"Oh, uh, yeah. I might have something," Gideon responded, pointing to the locker where he usually kept an extra outfit. When working with fire, it paid to keep an extra set on hand, just in case.

Flicking open his locker, she quickly rifled through its contents, pulling out a pair of sweatpants and an old t-shirt. Holding up the pants to her waist, she murmured something about them doing for the time being.

As she slid her legs into the pants, Gideon realized that he was staring again, so he turned his back to give her privacy. "You can keep the clothes," he offered.

Dacey chuckled lightly. "Nah, sweatpants aren't my normal style."

"Are you an angel?" Gideon asked. At Dacey's amused snort, he swallowed thickly and asked, "Demon?"

Dacey scoffed but didn't answer, leaving Gideon adrift in awkwardness. He stared at the old, stained wood paneled wall in front of him and tried to find a topic of discussion.

"Hey, so, um, I think you were murdered?" Gideon said, although the words came out as a question. He couldn't stop picturing her slit throat. "Do you know who killed you? Should I call the police?"

The woman laughed so loudly that Gideon whirled back to face her. Thankfully, she'd gotten fully dressed, so Gideon didn't need to avert his gaze anymore. Despite the grim situation they found themselves in, a hint of a smile tugged at the corner of Gideon's mouth as he watched Dacey, with determined focus, roll up the legs of the borrowed pants; a necessary adjustment given the noticeable height difference between them.

Dacey shook her head at Gideon, smirking. "Yeah, let's not

call the police. I just need to make a quick phone call first and then I'll be out of your hair."

"Wait. What am I supposed to tell everyone?"

The woman laughed again, a little bit of an incredulous edge to the sound. "What are you talking about? Don't tell anyone about this – unless you'd like to end up in the psych ward. No one will believe you."

Gideon knew that from experience. His shoulders dropped in defeat. "You're right. If I told anyone that a woman with wings made of fire came out of the incinerator, I'd end up getting committed again."

Dacey, who had turned away and was striding towards the exit, stopped, tension vibrating her frame. Then she whipped around and stared Gideon down. "What did you just say?"

CHAPTER 3

She quickly strode back to Gideon, staring at him with an intensity that left him rattled. "Uh, I was just saying that you're right. No one would believe me if I told them about you."

"Not that. The other thing. What did you see that was unusual about me?"

Gideon gave her an incredulous look. "You mean other than you crawling naked out of the incinerator when you should have been nothing but ashes?"

"Yeah, other than that." Gideon could feel the unspoken 'smart ass' tacked onto the end of Dacey's droll statement.

"You had wings sprouting from your back that were made of fire." Gideon dropped his face into his hands. His legs felt shaky, so he slid down and sat on the floor, putting his head between his knees. "God, what if this isn't real? What if I've lost it for good this time? My mom's going to be heartbroken. I can't do this to her again." He wanted to cry but refused to in front of the beautiful but tough woman – even if she was just a figment of his imagination.

Dacey blew out a slow breath, then sat next to Gideon. "Hey, you're okay, alright? This seems like a lot, but I need you to pull yourself together and help me out here. I'm sorry I was being a bit of a bitch – it's just being murdered and waking up in an oven always puts me in a bad mood."

Her words startled a chuckle out of Gideon. How often did she wake up like this? He peeked over at Candace's face, trying to figure out if she was kidding.

Gideon dropped his forehead back to his knees but turned his head slightly so he could keep watching Dacey. She was biting her lip, looking like she was mulling over something.

She looked over and caught Gideon staring at her. "Do you have a phone here I can use? I need to make some calls."

"You need to call George?" Gideon asked, a little jealous for no good reason.

"Yeah, among others."

Gideon heaved himself to his feet. "Sure. We have a phone in the front office you can use."

Dacey threw herself into Mr. Peterson's office chair in a way that made Gideon smile. His boss was a jerk about not letting anyone use his desk or any of his office supplies. Gideon's work-station was a cheap desk without a chair that he had to share with everyone else.

Picking up the phone and dialing a number, Dacey propped her bare feet on the desk, crossing one ankle over the other and stretching back into the chair, staring up at the ceiling. She leaned so far back in the chair that it creaked and tilted dangerously.

A phone started ringing from the shelf where they stored clients' personal belongings. Dacey thumped the chair back on the floor so fast that it screeched against the linoleum. She dropped the receiver on the desk, letting it continue to ring. Stalking over to the shelf, Dacey stared at the box where the sound was originating from.

Gideon heard her murmur, "Shit," quietly before yanking the

container off the shelf and taking it back to Mr. Peterson's desk. She stared down into the box's depths before turning back to Gideon.

"What is this?" Dacey asked in a way that implied she had already figured it out but needed to hear it out loud.

"Um, sometimes we are given our clients' personal items. We hold them until a family member claims them."

"You cremate any guys named George tonight?"

"No, but, um… My shift isn't over yet," Gideon said slowly, trying not to cringe.

"Damn it," Dacey said. Her shoulders dropped in a way that made Gideon want to give her a hug. Before he could, she looked up from the contents of the box and locked eyes with him, anchoring him to the spot. "What was your name again?"

"Um, Gideon."

"Alright, Um-Gideon, where do you store the bodies?"

Gideon turned and waved her to follow. "I'll show you."

He led Dacey to the refrigerator room. A rush of cold air swept over Gideon, raising goosebumps on his arms when he opened the door. Inside the fridge, the only sound was the soft whirring of the fan and the ping of the compressor cycling on. With a heavy heart, Gideon indicated the few remaining boxes nestled in the fridge that were still on his roster to process. Checking over the paperwork, he quickly located a box containing a man named George Norcia.

This body was also loosely wrapped in white cloth. Dacey slowly parted the cloth, uncovering the corpse's face. Gideon was surprised to see an older man. He had somehow expected someone closer to Dacey's age – someone in their late twenties – not a man nearing retirement age. Bruises painted his face, telling the tale of whatever violent encounter had ended his and Dacey's lives. Gideon was further surprised by George's clothing. He had expected something casual like Dacey's sundress. Instead, the man was clad in an expensive-looking suit, complete with a silken tie and pocket square. The outfit, once sharp and professional, was now torn and stained. His salt-and-pepper hair was snarled with dried blood and dirt, adding an element of disarray to his once-neat appearance.

Dacey made a quiet sound of either rage or shock – Gideon couldn't tell. She tugged the white shroud further out of the way, revealing more of the man's blood-soaked dress shirt, and a gruesome bullet wound in the middle of his chest.

Dacey peeled back his crimson-stained shirt so the full extent of the injury was laid bare. A stark halo of dried blood surrounded the dark, gaping wound, its jagged edges speaking of the sheer force that had torn through flesh and bone.

Gideon surreptitiously glanced over at Dacey, worried about how she was taking the death of her friend. She stood stock-still, staring at the dead man, her face unreadable. He sensed that she was hurting but hiding it behind a stoic mask. The room filled with an air of solemnity, a mix of grief and unanswered questions that lingered like a heavy fog. With a gentle touch on Dacey's tense shoulder, Gideon offered silent support.

Gideon pulled away when Dacey shrugged off his touch and let loose a litany of curse words that would have made a trucker blush. She had what Gideon's mother would call 'salty' language.

"George, you stupid asshole. I told you not to come with me. Why didn't you run? I can regenerate, you idiot."

Dacey whirled on her heels and stalked out of the walk-in fridge. Gideon replaced the lid on George's cremation box and scurried after her.

"I'd like to see my and George's paperwork. Can you show me where you keep the records?" Dacey asked when he emerged from the refrigerator.

Without comment, Gideon pointed to the station where they kept the files and forms. Quickly scanning through the stack of folders, she grabbed two from the pile. Then, Dacey turned and stalked away, already absorbed in the documents.

He caught up to her as she returned to the front office. Her shoulders were tense, held high and rigid, as if ready for a confrontation. Restless rage emanated from her as she paced back and forth, her movements quick and jerky. Her brows furrowed as she read over the paperwork. Her lips were pressed tightly together, forming a thin line, while her jaw clenched with every exhale. Gideon was a little worried that she was moments from snapping. Her eyes, with their fiery center, glowed hotter with an angry intensity. Dacey's entire being seemed to radiate an energy that made it clear that any attempt at calm discussion would be useless.

"There's nothing for it. I gotta call Headquarters. Shit," Dacey growled. She pinched the bridge of her nose as if trying to stave off a headache.

Plopping back into Mr. Peterson's chair, Dacey dialed a number and drummed her nails against the fake wood top of the desk.

Someone must've answered, despite the late hour, because Dacey straightened abruptly in the chair. "Dacey Menet checking in. Things went south. My handler is dead, and I woke up inside a crematorium oven." Dacey paused, listening to whoever was on the other end of the call. "Yeah, it all went tits up. The target either sensed I was coming, or he was tipped off. Can you get Trina to investigate whether the target was warned or if I just got sloppy? I don't see how; I was careful – took all the usual precautions. I didn't even get a good look at his face. He shouldn't have been expecting me – I was careful. Also, I somehow ended up in the wrong crematorium. Just about made the guy working here piss his pants. I'm going to be following up on that personally. What if I had ended up in the ground instead of an oven?"

Dacey ran her hand through her hair, pulling at the strands in frustration.

"Yeah, I'm pretty sure I'm still in Florida's armpit." The was a small pause. "No. I'm certain I'm still in the Panhandle. I can smell the ocean." She gave Gideon's Gulf Breeze Zoo t-shirt a pointed look. With another pause, she placed her hand over the receiver. "Hey, Gideon, where exactly are we?"

"Uh, Peterson Cremation Services," Gideon again explained.

"No shit, Sherlock." Dacey tempered her words with a teasing grin. "I'm aware of that. What *town* am I in?"

Gideon gave her a sheepish look. "Sorry. You're in Gulf Breeze."

Dacey repeated that into the receiver. "Yeah, not too far from where I died. Oh, him? That's Um-Gideon. He's the crematorium employee I frightened. And I think he's an auramancer. Yeah... a sensate, I swear."

An auramancer? Sensate? What the hell was that? Something about the way Dacey said the words made his stomach drop.

"I'm going to need a new handler. See who is available – anybody but MacGuire. That guy gets on my nerves. In the meantime, can you have a new kit bag sent to my hotel? Also, we need a team to pick up George's body. I'll text you the address. I need to get back after my target. Have HR start the paperwork to get his wife the death benefits as soon as possible. Don't worry, I'll call Isabel and let her know what happened. It's the least I can do. I'll call back once I have more info."

Once Dacey hung up the phone, she speared Gideon with an intense scrutinizing look. Something about the way she looked at him – the way a scientist might an interesting bug specimen – made him want to take a step back. "Tell me, Um-Gideon. Besides tonight, with my resurrection and my wings, you ever see anything strange? Something no one else could; something you couldn't explain?"

Gideon gave an emphatic, almost frantic shake of his head. Dacey stared at him, stopping to pick at a cuticle. Without looking up from the examination of her nail, Dacey said, "I think you're lying to me. In fact, I'm certain you are."

CHAPTER 4

"Ɉ don't know what you're talking about. I'm not lying," Gideon stammered. He could feel a telltale blush work its way up his neck. For the hundredth time, he wished that he wasn't so pale. If he had the ability to tan, it would hide how embarrassingly easily he blushed.

Gideon opened his mouth to further argue, but Dacey gave him a droll look, waving away his attempt to continue the lie.

"Let me take a stab at this." She gave him a long, head-to-toe perusal. "This is not the first time you've seen something you can't explain. I bet you told someone about seeing monsters when you were little. People admonished you to stop making up stories and tall tales – probably your parents or perhaps your teachers – so you started to keep what you were seeing to your-self. Or maybe you spent a lot of time with therapists who told you that what you were seeing wasn't real. You're probably very familiar with being medicated. Wait… you said something about not wanting to be committed again. So, I'd bet that you saw something and told someone or freaked out in public, and that landed you in a psychiatric facility. So now you hide here, working a graveyard shift at a crematorium where it keeps you away from people and from seeing things you can't explain. How am I doing? Anywhere close to the truth?"

The analysis pissed him off – no one likes being put under a microscope. But it was especially uncomfortable because Dacey had come unsettlingly close to the truth. After his glare bounced harmlessly off Dacey, Gideon gave a defeated sigh. He'd vowed never to talk about this again, but… if she was a figment of his imagination, there was no one besides the dead bodies to over-hear his confession.

"You got most of that right," said Gideon. "You missed your calling as a carnival barker. When I was little, I told my mom and the pastor at church. I think they were planning to perform an exorcism, but I had just seen *The Exorcist* at a sleepover, and it freaked me out so badly that I told everyone that I had been faking it all for attention. I swear, the preacher was disappointed that he didn't get to perform an exorcism on me, so I stand by my choice to lie. So, yes, I learned how to ignore things I couldn't explain. However, when I was in college, I saw one of my professors attack and bite a classmate's throat. I called the police and accused a teacher of murder, screaming about him ripping out a girl's throat with his teeth. Imagine my surprise when the victim was found and turned out to be completely fine. I found myself on a 72-hour hold at a psychiatric facility after that. It ended with me losing my scholarship and being given a restraining order. I couldn't afford the tuition anymore, and everyone treated me like I was deranged."

"What did your family say about what happened? Do any of them also get 'hallucinations'?"

"It's only me and my mom. And I lied about why I had to leave college. I told her that I couldn't handle the pressure. I was never very good in school anyway, so she believed me. I just couldn't bring myself to tell her that I was hallucinating and falsely accused a professor of murder. It would have broken her heart to find out that I'd gotten myself Baker Acted."

Dacey nodded as if Gideon's personal tragedy made sense and was no big deal. That incident had left a hole in his life like a smoking crater. He lost his girlfriend, his job, his education, and the future he'd mapped out for himself. It had permanently altered the trajectory of his entire life. It had been years ago, and his mom still treated him with kid gloves, perpetually worried about his stress levels. She tiptoed around his emotions as if scared that any misstep would tumble him back into that dark time.

To find out that what he'd witnessed had probably been real was a gut punch. It also made him want to go find Professor Blackwood and put a stake through his heart. Blackwood let Gideon destroy his life when he'd known the truth.

Shaking off the 'what could have beens', Gideon looked at Dacey seriously. "What's an oralmancer? Or a sensate? Or whatever it was that you call me."

Instead of answering, Dacey stood up and approached the shelves where personal belongings were stored. She scanned the labels on the containers, walking down the line. "There it is," Dacey announced, pulling a box off the shelf, and dropping it next to George's box on Mr. Peterson's desk.

Tossing aside the lid, she quickly rifled through the box's contents. The scowl forming on her face didn't suggest good things. "Damn it. They must've confiscated my weapons. I swear, this night. Could it get any worse?"

Peeking over Dacey's shoulder, Gideon watched as she grabbed a small purse and checked its contents. She pulled out a set of keys, then feathered through a wallet before slipping both items into her pocket. The only other item in the box was a shiny newer-model phone.

Dacey turned, catching Gideon snooping. He gave her a shrug and a repentant look, but she wasn't paying attention to that. Gideon followed her as she headed through the door that led to the back half of the crematorium.

"Come on. We need to deal with George," Dacey called.

"What did you mean 'deal with George'?" he asked Dacey, riddled with curiosity and a smidge of concern.

Dacey glanced at him, her fiery eyes softening marginally. "We need to make sure George doesn't end up being cremated like I was, Gideon. I will be sending for a retrieval team, but it might take a few hours until they get here. We need to secure him until they arrive."

Nodding slowly in understanding, Gideon followed Dacey to the fridge. Together, they removed the tags and paperwork from the box that housed George's body, relocating him to the shadows of an isolated back corner. They worked silently and diligently, the quiet punctuated only by the distant hum of the crematorium's machinery.

Once finished, Gideon, feeling slightly breathless and on edge, turned towards Dacey. "If your retrieval team isn't going to get here for a few hours, the day shift will be here at that point. I don't know how they'll be able to get the body without raising a lot of questions."

Dacey only shrugged in response, an enigmatic smile gracing her features. "The retrieval team will tie up any loose ends and can easily deal with your co-workers. It won't be a problem – they do this kind of stuff all the time," she responded dismissively, meeting his worried stare with a reassuring one of her own. "We've done good, Gideon. George's body is safe for now, and that's what matters."

Leaving behind the fridge, Dacey headed back to the front room. Gideon had to rush to keep up with her brisk stride. Once she reached the receiving room, Dacey stopped in her tracks and Gideon almost plowed into her back.

"I need your car keys."

Dacey's order hung heavily in the air, the tension thickening between them. Gideon stared at her, taken aback by her demand.

"No. Absolutely not. I'm sorry, but no. I understand that you need a ride, but just call an Uber or something, like a normal person. I need my car to get home and to my other job."

But Dacey seemed unmoved by his plea. "I'm taking those keys whether you hand them to me or not. I need to track down the guy who killed me and George before he gets to anyone else. Time is of the essence here. My needs trump yours. So I'm sorry about your second job but I need your car. However… you can come with me. I can tell you what an auramancer is and why I think you are one."

"Those choices suck," Gideon informed her with a roll of his eyes. He got the sense that Dacey was angling to try and get him to come with her.

At that moment, Gideon felt torn between his sense of self-preservation and a lingering curiosity that sparked within him. He'd always thought that he was crazy – to find out that there might be an explanation for the occasional hallucinations he experienced was very tempting. A whirlwind of thoughts swirled in his head, shuffling through the risks and consequences of each option. Yet, something in Dacey's fire-ringed eyes hinted at a greater purpose, something bigger than he ever imagined.

"Come on…" Dacey wheedled. "It'll be fun."

"Fun."

However, despite his protests, Gideon shoved his hand in his pocket and pulled out his car keys. When Dacey reached for them, he held them up above her head, his hand tightened around the keychain, his knuckles turning white. With a deep breath, he made his choice, his voice firm as he uttered the words, "Fine, let's go."

"I'm driving," Dacey demanded, jumping and trying to snag the keys still dangling in Gideon's grip. He jerked them up higher, keeping them out of reach. The fiery ring around her pupil flashed, showing her annoyance. When Dacey bared her teeth at him like a wild creature ready to attack, Gideon had to swallow a laugh. She seemed as fierce as an angry kitten, but he wisely didn't point that out to her.

She tried to jump and snatch the keys from his hands again, but he was at least seven inches taller than her and jerked them out of her reach.

"Don't make me hurt you. I'm driving. Give them to me," Dacey growled at him.

"No, you're not. It's my car – I'm driving." When he saw her gearing up for more arguing, he shook his head. "You will have to pry these keys from my cold dead hands."

"That can be arranged." Dacey looked tempted by the idea but finally huffed out a resigned sigh. "Fine, Um-Gideon. Whatever. You can drive. Now let's go."

Gideon started to turn away when he saw a smile start to break through Dacey's scowl. He got the impression that she was having fun – or perhaps she was just a little crazy.

Dacey grabbed the boxes holding her and George's belongings before turning on her heel and heading for the front door. Gideon stared after her stupidly for a moment before shaking his head at himself. "Wait! Hold on. I can't go yet. I need to finish my shift."

Dacey whirled back at him, giving Gideon a patient look that appeared a little frayed around the edges. "Dude. We've been over this. I need to go and catch my killer now. Right now. Forget your job, Gideon! Who cares about this place?"

"This place is how I pay my bills."

She gave him an understanding look. "Okay. How 'bout this? Tell your boss that a family emergency came up, and if you help me, I'll give you a portion of what would have been George's cut. I can't give it all to you, however. I need to save some for his wife. But it will more than make up for any wages you might lose tonight."

Fresh out of easy excuses, Gideon wrote a quick note and left it on Mr. Peterson's desk before following Dacey out the front door, locking it behind him.

Dacey was on her cell phone when he approached. She dipped her chin in thanks as she slipped into the vehicle. "Yeah, I'm headed back now. Text me when my new kit bag arrives, okay? Also, see if the Numerai can get access to the police reports for my and George's murders. Get me everything. I want to know if the police have any ideas about the killer. Okay, thanks; I'll call when I have news."

Getting behind the wheel, he glanced over to ask Dacey where to go when he caught her grimacing at his car's worn interior in distaste. The dash was bleached from the relentless Florida sun and the upholstery was cracked and faded. "You're welcome to walk if this isn't up to your usual standards, princess."

Dacey chuckled, giving Gideon an approving smirk. "Oh ho ho. Look who found his spine! I like it."

Gideon shook away his answering grin. "Okay, where to?"

Turning her attention back to the paperwork clutched in her hand, Dacey murmured distractedly, "Head to Niceville." Curiosity piqued, Gideon raised an eyebrow, stealing a quick glance at the woman beside him. However, she paid him no mind. She was focused on the cremation paperwork. With just a quick glance, Gideon recognized the death certificate form in her hand.

Starting his car, Gideon pulled out on the Gulf Breeze Parkway, heading east as requested. "What's in Niceville?"

The name conjured images of idyllic charm, serenity, and pleasant people, but Gideon knew that it was just a small coastal college town like any other. Based on the wrinkle to Dacey's nose and the curl of her lip, Niceville wasn't living up to its moniker.

"Northwest Florida State's campus. Where several students have died, and a few have gone missing recently. Normally, I wouldn't be called in for something like this, but most of the kids had magic of one variety or another."

Magic? Gideon thought incredulously but before he could start asking questions, Dacey continued, "All the police reports stated that they were drug addicts and runaways, but there are more people dead and missing than normal for a campus of that size. Plus, two of the missing persons' families are very adamant that their children would never fall victim to drug addiction, and after looking into their lives, I would agree. It got flagged in the system, so I got sent to follow up. Several of the victims disappeared after spending an evening at one of the restaurants and bars near the water, so I spent an evening out alone pretending to drink too much. The last thing I remember was getting attacked near Plew Lake. The guy hit me like a freight train. We got into a fight, and he somehow bested me which, even if he caught me by surprise, is no easy feat."

"You said that you got 'sent' to follow up. Does that mean you work for the government?"

"You could say that. I'm a subcontractor for a regional government agency that you've never heard of. I'm a fixer."

"That doesn't make any sense. And it doesn't really answer my question. And don't fixers work for the mafia or something?"

"It's the best that you're going to get. And, no, I don't work for the mob, so you can stop clutching your pearls." The paper in Dacey's hand crinkled as she emitted a startled sound. "This says my cause of death was an overdose. Holy shit – that's a first. The guy must've knocked me out and then administered some sort of drug. I'll be interested to see what my toxicology report turns up."

Gideon gulped, his hands automatically tightening on the steering wheel. "That doesn't make any sense. When you came in, I got a look at your injuries – your throat had been slashed. You might have overdosed, but I'm pretty sure your cause of death was blood loss from the wound across your neck."

A silence filled the car before Dacey turned fully in her seat to face Gideon. "How sure are you about the cause of my death? I need you to be certain before I open this can of worms."

"It was a gaping wound across your entire neck. I could see the inside of your esophagus. I'm as certain as you can get."

"Well, shit. I need to make some more calls."

CHAPTER 5

Several phone calls – and a lot of cussing – later, Dacey was fuming. Gideon had to turn up the air conditioning because the inside of the car had started to get overly warm. Gideon was pretty sure that the rise in temperature was coming from Dacey, but wisely refrained from asking about it. Sparks were crackling in her hair, making the strands look alive.

"Let's review the facts," Dacey said, counting off the issues on her fingers. "My target was somehow able to subdue and kill me. Then he killed my handler. I ended up at the wrong crematorium. The death certificate doesn't reflect my actual cause of death. It's also backdated to two days ago, stating that my 'autopsy' was conducted Monday night. However, I was in Tallahassee then – and alive. The cremation authorization was signed off, but the sheriff who signed off on it obviously didn't wait the mandatory 48 hours since I was murdered last night. Not to mention that, as a murder victim, it shouldn't have been done at all. Same with George's authorization – it should have been Isabel as his next of kin, who should have signed off on that, but somehow it lists that he doesn't have next of kin to authorize. I don't know exactly what is happening here, but after we check the crime scene, I need to find the police officer who handled this case."

"Um, if a cop was involved do you think they will recognize you if you show up in their office? Seeing someone who was previously dead might raise some questions."

"Hmm, good point. Let me think about how to handle that. I think I'm just rattled that someone got the drop on me. Pretty pissed about getting my throat cut."

Getting angry wasn't how Gideon imagined most people reacted to dying, but Dacey didn't seem like most people. "How exactly did you survive that? You don't even have a scar to show for it. Are you… are you an angel?"

Dacey snorted. "You keep asking me that. For the last time, I'm not an angel, I promise. Try again."

Gideon thought about her wings made of fire. He cut his eyes from the road to look at her profile as she gazed absently out at the beach to their right. He hesitated but then decided to bulldoze his way through. "And you're not a demon?"

Dacey giggled. "My high school teachers probably thought so, but no." She hesitated, the smile dropping from her face. "I'm a bennu shifter."

"A what?"

Dacey picked at her fingernails like she wanted to avoid the conversation, but then with a sigh she looked directly at Gideon with a hint of defiance. She folded her hands in her lap, leaning back with a small sigh, "Ever heard of the sun deity Ra, Gideon?"

Gideon blinked, trying to recall anything he'd heard of Ra – he didn't want to admit that most of what he knew came from movies. "Uh, it's some sort of Egyptian god, right?"

She nodded, a ghost of a smile appearing on her face. "Ra is considered the chief deity in ancient Egyptian mythology. He was a falcon-headed god that was associated with the sun, creation, and life. He was a very old and revered deity. The bennu was believed to be the spirit or soul of Ra, the sun god, made flesh on Earth in the form of a heron."

He glanced away from the road and squinted at Dacey, processing the fact that this fierce, fiery woman was relating her origins to a bird-god. It was absolutely mind-boggling, but he tried to keep up. "Heron, like, a big crane bird?"

"Exactly," she said, grinning. "The bennu symbolized creation, renewal, and rebirth. It was considered the bringer of light and a symbol of the new dawn. It was also said to have lived for five hundred years before bursting into flame, only to rise anew from the ashes, much like a—"

"A phoenix?" Gideon interjected with sudden comprehension. He felt excitement surge through him. That would explain the fire, her wings, and her survival.

Dacey smiled. "Indeed. My people believe that the Greeks and Romans used the bennu to create their own myths of the phoenix. Over time, the myths merged, and the bennu became synonymous with the phoenix. I prefer the term bennu because I can transform into a heron, so that name is more accurate."

Gideon remained silent, his mouth hanging open, his gaze fixated on Dacey. His mind struggling to grasp the enormity of her revelation. He found himself continually switching his attention from the road before them to the enigmatic woman in the passenger seat. He had heard tales of the fabled phoenix, a creature of myth said to be reborn from its own ashes. But to have the living embodiment of that very legend sitting next to him inside his ancient Corolla just didn't compute.

"Um, the bennu is a bird, and you're… you," Gideon said, then immediately wished he hadn't . Obviously, that couldn't be true since the woman sitting next to him was clearly a human.

Thankfully, Dacey ignored his inane words. Instead, she continued to explain, "As a bennu shifter, I possess certain abilities. I have the power of regeneration – as you saw. When I die, if my body is set on fire, I am reborn with my wounds healed and my strength restored." Gideon could almost detect a flicker of flames dancing in her eyes, like she was a creature made from fire, not just regenerated by it. "My strength and speed surpass that of typical humans. Fire does not burn me, and I don't get overheated – which is great for living in the South. I am obviously not a bird, but my fire wings can carry me for short distances. And when I unleash my power, I can burn things with my touch. Also, I can transform into a heron."

Gideon swallowed thickly, trying to process Dacey's words. "You mean like… like a werewolf?"

"Yes. And, no, I won't show you. So don't ask."

Gideon's mind reeled, grappling with the realization that he was within touching distance of a creature steeped in myth and legend, a being capable of defying death itself.

"Also, if you tell anyone about me, I'll show you just how effective my power over fire is. If you betray me, you'll be nothing more than a smoking husk by the time I finish with you. Got it?"

Gideon made a sound that was half indignation and half dismay. He felt like they'd already been through so much together, so to hear that Dacey thought he might betray her disappointed him. "Hey, your secret is safe with me. I won't tell a soul, I promise."

"You better not," was Dacey's murmured response.

"Does that mean that you'll live to be five hundred years old? Or that you'll live forever?" Gideon glanced at Dacey out of the corner of his eyes, wondering if she was perhaps much older than she appeared. It made him think of Methuselah from his youth bible study classes.

"Nope, I'll live a normal life span. One day, someone will put me on a funeral pyre, and I'll just burn up and not return. Bennu shifters all die of natural causes."

"So… what happens when you die? You know, before you're

brought back? Do you, like, see the afterlife? The light at the end of the tunnel, or your grandmother waving you on?"

Dacey chuckled. "No, I wish. There's just nothing, a blank void, then I'm waking up on fire."

Silence settled over the car while Gideon mulled over the thought that mythical creatures like the bennu truly existed. If they were real, what else was out there?

Finally, Gideon couldn't stand the silence anymore. He normally reveled in the quiet, but there were too many questions clamoring inside his brain. Dacey glanced at him sharply when he cleared his throat. He chewed on his lip, trying to work up the courage to ask, when Dacey lost her patience and snapped, "What? What is going on over there with you?"

"I was wondering… Since we've established that bennus are real… Uh, are there other magical creatures that are real? You know, like vampires?" Gideon asked, thinking back to the professor he'd witnessed biting that co-ed.

"Yep, there sure are. Pretty much any creature of legend or with magical powers – they exist. We're called Mythicals. And this world is filled with them."

"So, like, vampires are real?"

"Yep. *Like, totally.*"

Gideon knew that she was teasing him, but he was too overwhelmed to feel embarrassed. Who cared if he tended to stutter and add 'like' or 'um' to every other word when he was nervous or excited?

"You're a brat," Gideon informed Dacey who only grinned unrepentantly at his words. "What about werewolves? Leprechauns? Mermaids? Are they real?"

"Yep, yep, yep. All real. Witches, gnomes, fae, dragons – all of them exist."

"Okay. What about the Swamp Ape? Is he real?"

Dacey started laughing. "What the hell is a Swamp Ape? I've never heard of that. And I thought I'd heard it all."

"You know, the Swamp Ape. It's like our local Bigfoot. Oh my god! Is Bigfoot real?" Gideon laughed in delight before Dacey could even answer. "I can't believe magical creatures are real."

As fast as the humor hit him, it died. This meant that he wasn't crazy. That he'd never been hallucinating. That sobered Gideon right up. He shook his head in denial.

"Well, you are one," Dacey said. "You're an auramancer. A sensate. What I can't believe is how you got to be an adult, and no one ever noticed or told you."

A small piece of Gideon didn't want to ask; staying ignorant would make his life easier. But hadn't he daydreamed of adventure? He'd just been scared that he'd end up committed again if he reached too far. When he kept his world small and repetitive, he kept it safe and sane.

"What does that mean exactly? What is an auramancer, and why do you think I am one?"

"Auramancers, or sensates, are rare. They're people with the ability to perceive magic. I've heard that auramancers have heightened senses attuned to the subtle vibrations of magic, or anything supernatural. With practice, you should even be able to see through glamors. Even those creatures adorned with sigil tattoos or concealed under enchantments cannot hide their true forms from a well-trained sensate. I've heard of auramancers who could see people's actual souls, another that could see ley lines, and I've even heard rumors of a woman who can detect ghosts and spirits. It is as if you possess a sixth sense, granting you a glimpse into a hidden world others can only imagine. *And* you guys are supposed to be almost immune to most magic, so spells don't always work on you. You're gonna be able to make bank once you're trained."

Gideon gulped, not sure how he felt about being an auramancer. Although the idea of *making 'bank'* was very appealing. If he could start making decent money, he could help his mom more. Maybe even get her a new washing machine.

Shaking his head out of daydreams about new appliances, he glanced at Dacey out of the corner of his eye. "And you're certain that I'm an auramancer – a sensate?"

"You saw my wings. That shouldn't have been possible. I have a sigil tattoo to make me appear completely human, even when they're spread. I should've just looked like a regular naked woman climbing out of the incinerator. Tell me... is there anything different about my eyes?"

"You have a small ring of fire around your pupil. When you're pissed off, they burn brighter."

"Huh, do they now?" Dacey murmured as if that was news to her.

"Why can't I see your wings anymore? If I'm an auramancer, shouldn't I be able to see them?"

"Oh, yeah. I put the fire out and I retracted them."

"Huh," was all Gideon could think to say.

CHAPTER 6

Silence had fallen between Gideon and Dacey, and they'd been driving almost thirty minutes that way. As the sky slowly started to lighten with dawn, Dacey's phone rang.

"Hey, Wiz, whatcha got for me?"

Gideon tried to listen in but could only detect a feminine voice on the other end of the line.

"You got 'em? Excellent. Email them to me. Because I gotta tell ya – something is not adding up here. The police officer who filled out my death certificate, Officer Kaminski, has some questions to answer. Can you have his background pulled? Oh, and the coroner who signed off on my death certificate, too."

Dacey hung up the call and opened her email to read.

"We're almost to Niceville," Gideon said. "Where exactly do you want me to go?"

"I need shoes," Dacey replied, lifting one of her legs and wiggling her bare toes at Gideon. He was bemused to see her toenails were painted a summery peach-pink. It seemed at odds with her bad-ass persona. Although, she *had* been wearing a feminine summer dress when he'd put her into the oven. He wanted to comment and tease Dacey, but he wasn't sure whether she'd laugh along or punch him in the mouth. It felt like it could go either way with the mercurial woman.

Dacey pointed towards a small convenience store crowding the road they were on. "Oh, over there! That store has some beach stuff in the window. I bet they have flip-flops."

As Gideon pulled the car into the gas station's parking lot, Dacey's eyes brightened at the display of brightly patterned sarongs, swimsuits, and towels filling the front window. "I need to blend in," she said to Gideon.

Inside, Dacey made a beeline for the aisle stuffed with beach gear, scanning the racks. She grabbed a simple pair of cheap foam flip-flops, their vibrant color contrasting with her gruff demeanor. Moving swiftly, she made her way to the accessories section, where she picked up a beachy straw hat and a pair of sunglasses. She slipped them on, stuffed her hair into the hat, and gave Gideon a mischievous grin. She made a quick stop in the candy aisle and grabbed some M&Ms.

The hat covered Dacey's thick wavy hair, and the sunglasses shielded her fiery, piercing gaze. Though she still exuded an air of power and confidence, the disguise gave her an added layer of anonymity. "Let's get back on the road," she said. "We're going to retrace my steps from last night, so let's head to the Ruby Tuesday on John Sims Parkway."

Following his phone's directions, he watched out of the corner of his eyes as Dacey picked out all the red and orange M&Ms and ate them first. She offered Gideon all the blue ones which he happily accepted.

Gideon pulled his car into the chain restaurant's empty parking lot a few minutes later. The morning light highlighted the worn-out paint, revealing years of exposure to the scorching Florida sunshine. He hurriedly unbuckled his seatbelt and followed Dacey as she stepped out of the car, her determined stride leading her toward the front doors of the establishment.

She rattled the handle with annoyance; her face contorted in a mix of impatience and determination. "Man, I need some caffeine – my brain's totally scattered. I forgot it wouldn't be open this early. I'm hoping they have security cameras pointed toward the parking lot and street. Maybe we can get a look at our perp if I was followed," she explained. She gave Gideon a sour look. "We'll come back later."

Gideon glanced around the empty parking lot, his brow furrowing with concern. "How are you going to talk them into letting us see the footage?" At her imperiously raised eyebrow, Gideon decided not to question her further. "So… what now?" he asked instead.

"We're going to retrace my steps," she replied firmly, then she held out a hand to Gideon.

He stared at the offered palm in befuddlement, trying to understand what Dacey was asking. Normally, he'd think that she wanted to hold his hand. However, even after knowing her less than three hours, he was sure she wasn't the hand-in-hand strolling-together type. They stood in a strange standoff, Dacey with her hand outstretched and Gideon staring at it like it was a viper poised to strike. Finally, with a huff, Dacey snatched Gideon's hand into hers and laced her fingers with his.

Giving him a tug, she turned them towards the sidewalk that was hugging the busy road. "Come on. We need to look like a couple. Our suspect only targets lone individuals. And could you try to look natural? You look like I've kidnapped you."

"I mean… you kind of have." As soon as the words were out of his mouth, Gideon desperately wished he could take them back, but Dacey just chuckled.

With a quick glance at Gideon, she added, "Keep an eye on the neighboring businesses. Maybe one of them has a camera pointed towards the road, and we can see if I was followed last night."

Together, they ventured down the road, occasionally stopping as if to admire a shop or get in a quick snuggle, but Dacey was checking their trail for any signs her assailant might have left behind.

They strolled down several blocks, heading deeper into the center of Niceville. Finally, they paused in front of a fried chicken shop while Dacey pretended to make a phone call. She gave Gideon a look, shading her eyes from the sun. "Okay, I want you to try to sense if you feel any magical residue. I know the guy is long gone, but he's gotta be a magical heavy hitter if he can take me down, so if we're lucky, you'll pick up on something."

"But I don't know how to do that."

Dacey bit her lip, nodding as she gave him a thoughtful stare. "Right. Let's… let's do an experiment. Close your eyes. Turn your awareness toward me and concentrate. Reach your senses out to me and tell me what you feel."

Gideon sighed, dread pooling in his gut. Dacey believed that he could do this, and he was about to let her down. It made a horrible gnawing start up inside his rib cage like even his own organs wanted to get away from him. Even his own guts thought he was a loser. He closed his eyes and tried to concentrate. He stood there for a minute, feeling like an idiot.

Opening his eyes, he gave Dacey an apologetic look. "I don't feel anything. I want to help, but I don't know how."

Dacey clenched her jaw and pursed her lips at him. "You're not really trying. Come on, dude. You're so scared you're going to get it wrong that you'd rather give up than really try. Now, close your eyes and try again. Stop being such a pu—"

Gideon held up a hand to stop the insult on the tip of Dacey's tongue. She rolled her eyes at him and then tried to give him an encouraging look. That somehow felt worse than the insults. "Just try, okay?"

Gideon dipped his chin and closed his eyes. He reminded himself that magic was real, and so were all the strange things he'd thought he'd been imagining for all these years. He thought he was crazy and had been trying to ignore anything that wasn't 'normal' for so long he didn't know how to stop. He'd been actively pushing away anything strange or magical for almost as long as he could remember. Dropping his mental shields made him feel naked and exposed.

Drawing in a slow breath, Gideon held it, and then as he exhaled, he tried to push his awareness out. He knew where Dacey was standing, less than two feet to his right, so he pushed his senses in that direction.

When he felt something, it startled him so badly that he almost opened his eyes and lost the thread. "Holy shit. I sense heat. And like, I don't know, like a crackling energy. It's hard to describe. One time one of my friends bet me a dollar to lick a nine-volt battery. It feels like that – like sizzling energy."

"You licked a battery on a bet?"

Gideon opened his eyes and gave her a droll look. "Give me a break. I was in middle school."

Dacey flashed him a quick grin before getting a serious look on her face again. "This is progress. I want you to try again, but ignore me this time, push past my presence, and see what else you feel."

Gideon closed his eyes and tried again. The feeling of Dacey's bennu magic was strong and distracting. It felt like tingly warm flames licking over his skin, followed by a brush of something soft and delicate, almost like down feathers against his fingertips. Silently growling at himself to do better, he finally was able to push his senses past her. He didn't feel like he could get them more than ten or fifteen feet away from his body before awareness of his surroundings petered out.

Opening his eyes, Gideon shook his head at Dacey. "I can feel your magic, mostly. There are twinges of something faint around but I'm not even sure if I feel something or am just imagining it. And I can't sense very far – probably less than twenty feet."

"Okay, let's keep moving. My next stop was Honeybee Ice Cream. While we walk, I want you to keep your senses open. You'll get better the more you practice, like building a muscle."

CHAPTER 7

Gideon couldn't see the ice cream shop; it was hidden around a curve in the road ahead. According to Dacey, it was just over a block away. He knew that it wouldn't be open this time of day, but an ice cream cone sounded heavenly as the heat started to grow with the rising sun. Only in Florida would it be hot and muggy at seven in the morning, Gideon thought sourly.

He almost stumbled as a strange feeling washed over him. Dacey glanced at him sharply. "What's wrong?" she asked.

"I don't know," Gideon said slowly. "I think I feel something. It feels… dark maybe? It makes me feel a little nauseous… like I ate something rotten. It's hot too, but a different kind of heat than yours. It's definitely overlapping the trail your magic left, making it feel hotter."

"That's good. I'm no expert in magic auras, so that doesn't tell me much. There are lots of creatures that give off dark, malevolent magic. Maybe a necromancer or a shadow mage? Actually, maybe not a shadow mage, not if there's heat in the magical signature. Let's follow the trail and see where it leads."

Gideon tilted his head like a dog trying to track its prey. "I think it's following your path."

Dacey's aura led them on a meandering route as they retraced her fake-drunken steps from the night before. It quickly became clear that the second, darker aura had been following Dacey. However, where her path snaked and zigzagged as she had stopped in front of shop windows and other sights, pretending to be a drunk tourist, the other aura stayed in a straight line. The more Gideon fixated on the two magical trails, the more pronounced they became for him. Dacey's was vibrant and intense, – radiating a brilliant, fiery energy. In stark contrast, the other aura felt cloaked in foul darkness and foreboding energy, casting an eerie gloom wherever it went. Gideon also sensed that Dacey's pursuer had a masculine feel at odds with Dacey's feminine one.

He told her as much.

"Yeah, I'm pretty sure it was a man that attacked me. I wonder how far behind me he was," Dacey murmured when Gideon described what he was experiencing. "I can't believe I didn't notice a tail last night. Total amateur hour. If the team finds out, they're going to give me so much shit."

As they came abreast of the ice cream shop, a strange sensation tugged Gideon away from the sidewalk and towards the outside seating area. He pulled Dacey along with him, finally stopping next to an unoccupied picnic table with a bright, multi-colored umbrella. He stared at the empty seat for a moment, trying to parse the sensation.

"You picking something up?" Dacey asked.

"Yeah… I think. But this is different. It's more chaotic. Each time I feel like I can sense it, it changes on me. Reminds me of a… puppy? There's something mischievous about this aura."

Dacey gave Gideon such a pleased smile that he felt a blush creeping into his cheeks, which only got worse when she patronizingly patted his cheek. "Good job. You're already getting the hang of this. You're picking up on George's magic. He was sitting here, keeping an eye on me. He was a pooka, so it makes sense what you were picking up."

"Pooka?" Gideon repeated.

Dacey tugged Gideon to keep following the original path while she explained, "Yeah, so a pooka is a mythical creature, obviously. I think they originated in Ireland. They can shapeshift into a bunch of different animals, like dogs and horses and such, but they can also change their human appearance. It made him helpful in the field because he could scope out a situation or tail a perp without alerting them that they were on our radar.

"Pookas are also known for being mischievous. George loved playing tricks on people. The last time he pulled a prank on me, he Saran-Wrapped my entire desk at headquarters. Later, he confessed that he'd bought out the entire stock from Costco. It took me hours to saw through all that shit. I threatened that I would torch his favorite suit if he ever pulled another stunt like that one."

Gideon had a hard time imagining the man he'd seen being a practical joker. He had looked like he was dressed for an important board meeting. He didn't look like the type who enjoyed scaring people with fake bugs or putting bang snaps under a toilet seat.

Dacey's next words pulled Gideon out of his head. "Okay, just up ahead – see that bushy area? That's where I got grabbed and dragged into the woods. I don't remember much after that."

As they walked along the sidewalk, Dacey's gaze remained fixed on the dense thicket of bushy undergrowth crowding close to the sidewalk. As they drew nearer, she directed Gideon's attention to the disturbed bushes that lined the path. Broken branches and kicked-up dirt were sure signs of the recent struggle. Gideon's heart quickened with a mixture of anxiety and dread.

As Dacey stepped off the sidewalk and started heading into

the woods. She stopped abruptly when she realized that Gideon hadn't joined her. Returning to him, she tried to tug Gideon's arm to follow her, but he stood his ground, unmoved by her tugging or her grin.

"Come on, Gideon. It'll be fun!"

"Didn't you, like, get murdered in these woods?"

"Maybe," Dacey said with a shrug.

"You and I's definition of *fun* is very different," Gideon retorted. But despite his words, he stepped off the sidewalk and followed Dacey into the forest.

Following the twining aura trails and the telltale drag marks etched into the ground, they forged a path through the dense underbrush. Branches reached out like skeletal fingers, eager to snag onto passersby, scratching up Gideon's exposed arms. The sound of snapping twigs filled the air, punctuating their progress as they ventured deeper into the thicket. Gideon couldn't shake the growing sense of apprehension that crept up his spine, each rustle of foliage amplifying the tension within him.

Gideon swatted at yet another mosquito, grimacing at the itching bite that was sure to leave a welt on his exposed skin.

The woods around them were a quiet symphony of life, wrapped in a cocoon of tranquility. Old-growth cypress trees and ancient oaks held dominion over the landscape, their gnarled limbs stretched out like arms in a protective embrace. On them hung veils of Spanish moss like tattered, gray-green drapery. Beneath their strong trunks, palmetto leaves fanned out like brushstrokes on a canvas, and suffocating kudzu vines wrapped around trunks and laid over shrubs and deadwood. The blazing Florida sun tried in vain to penetrate this fortress, its brilliance reduced to a fragmented, dappled light that filtered down through the leafy canopy above. It painted the forest floor with a surreal, abstract quality, like a patchwork of stippled light and shadow. It was a scene filled with not only sights but sounds too, an underlying hum of buzzing cicadas, the sporadic rat-a-tat-tat of woodpeckers echoing in the treetops, and the chorus of crickets performing, their symphony resonating throughout the woods.

The deer trail they traversed widened, the undergrowth thinning and leaving them in a wooded glen. The once-untouched wilderness was now riddled with broken branches, their jagged edges pointing accusatory fingers at the unfolding mystery. Gideon looked around, trying to mentally recreate the scene. It was obvious to him that there had been a fight.

Gideon glanced over at Dacey to see how she was taking all this in.

"I'm okay. It's not the first time I've been murdered," Dacey said when she saw his worried expression. Gideon grimaced at her morbid humor, looking away from her fiery eyes and staring around the area.

"I'm just trying to help you figure out what happened here," he deflected.

The corners of Dacey's mouth quirked upwards into a smile, but it didn't reach her eyes.

"It all happened fast, but I remember being grabbed and dragged into the woods. It was dark, so I didn't get much of a look at the guy. He was dressed all in black, and he was bigger than me, but that's not saying much. We fought, but the struggle didn't last long… then nothing but darkness until I woke up in an oven." She absently rubbed the side of her head, as if trying to remember a phantom pain. She glanced at Gideon, a sense of insecurity peeking through her ember eyes. "I was knocked out. But…" She paused, brows furrowed in contemplation. "Not by a blow to the head or anything like that. I don't remember being hit. It felt different, like…" She glanced at him, her face was twisted in concentration as she tried to remember.

"Like the guy used some kind of spell or magic on me," she finally voiced. "So, either he has some type of power that can render someone unconscious, or he had a potion."

Gideon felt a chill run down his spine, his hands clenching tightly in nervous anticipation. His gaze dropped to the disturbed earth beneath their feet. Something bright and iridescent twinkled from under the scattered leaves. Gideon nudged Dacey's hand, pointing to the area then he crouched down to get a better look at it. He almost recoiled when he realized that it was mostly dried blood.

Dacey squatted down next to him. "Good spotting. I think that's mine. That means he didn't kill me here. There would be way more blood than this if he had."

Gideon couldn't look away from the scattered droplets of blood. "It shimmers."

Dacey turned and looked at Gideon in confusion. "What shimmers?"

"Your blood. It's like looking at a tiger-eye stone. There's fire in your blood."

"Huh. I guess that makes sense. I'm born from fire. I'm surprised that the fire is still visible once the blood leaves my body. You'd think that the magic would die after it's separated from the body. I need to look into that. Pays to know as much as possible," Dacey confided to Gideon.

Dacey straightened and gave the area a critical look. "Can you sense any new magic here? It might tell us how he managed to knock me out. He must've carried me out of here because I don't see any wheel tracks or anything."

Closing his eyes, Gideon sent his senses into the surrounding area. He immediately felt a disturbance in the middle of Dacey and her assailant's swirling magics. It was a void amidst the surrounding energies. Its presence invoked a sense of emptiness and a disorienting sensation akin to being adrift in an abyss.

When he tried to describe the feeling, Dacey assumed that the magic he was feeling was the magic her murderer used to knock her unconscious. She brushed aside the leaves in that area but couldn't find anything that would indicate what kind of spell the man used.

"Can you find where he took me?" Dacey asked in a hushed tone. A brief note of apprehension danced in the embers of her usually fiery gaze, revealing an unusual vulnerability.

Nodding, Gideon closed his eyes, reaching once more into the unseen world of energy that hummed and pulsed around them. Cutting through the haze of scattered auras, he focused on the dark threads of the man's aura, ignoring Dacey's fiery life force. There it weaved, a shadowy thread stretching out from the quiet hush of their current surroundings, leading away deeper into the forest.

"There," Gideon finally whispered, his voice shaky yet resolute. "It leads that way..." He pointed into the dense woods ahead of them.

Waving Dacey to follow him, Gideon let the invisible force tug at him, urging him further into the depths of the wilderness. The rustling of leaves and the entangled branches seemed to conspire against him, smacking against him as he followed the invisible path burning with dark, crackling energy in his mind.

With each step, Gideon's heart pounded in his chest, a mixture of anticipation and trepidation filling his veins. The path led him to another larger spot where the foliage was disturbed again, branches broken and crushed underfoot.

"I feel George's magic here," Gideon informed Dacey.

"Yeah, looks like signs of a much bigger fight," Dacey replied, walking around the area, staring at the ground and examining broken branches as if she understood the story they had to tell.

"George caught up to us, and the attacker dropped me here." Dacey indicated a broken and smooshed fern. "Then they fought. Look at these paw prints and claw marks. If I had to guess, I'd say that George transformed into a wolf. And then..." Dacey's words slowly died off as she walked across the ground slowly, stopping every few feet to examine the ground.

The atmosphere felt heavy with lingering tension as if the very air held echoes of a fierce battle.

"Look," Dacey said, squatting down and carefully sweeping away some brush and branches. "This is where he shot George. He tried to cover up the scene, but it's clear he was rushing. I imagine he never thought anyone would be looking for this."

Leaning over Dacey's shoulder, Gideon saw the pool of drying, congealing blood. The crimson stain had seeped into the ground.

Gideon pushed out his senses as hard as possible, suddenly feeling very exposed and vulnerable. They were alone in the middle of the woods, examining a murder scene. No one would be able to find them here if something awful happened. No one would hear their cries for help.

He reached for the killer's brand of magic, pushing his consciousness out to its limits, and breathed a small, silent sigh of relief when he didn't find anything else other than the man's trail leading away from the crime scene.

Dacey stood up and looked at Gideon.

"Can you still pick up his path and figure out where he took me?"

Dacey gave him such a determined, hopeful look, as if he was the key to all the answers she sought, that he knew he would do anything to keep from letting her down. Despite his growing trepidation, Gideon couldn't help but be drawn into this new world of uncertainty and magic, his own curiosity mingling with a rising sense of unease.

Gideon dipped his chin. He would see this through – wherever it took him.

CHAPTER 8

"Wherever it took him" turned out to be a parking lot.

Stopping just before they emerged from the dense woods, Dacey and Gideon found themselves staring at a sprawling parking lot that served a nearby golf course. Their eyes were immediately drawn to the large pro shop building that dominated the landscape with rolling pristine hills of green behind it. There were less than a dozen cars parked, most of them located either near the front door of the pro shop or under the shade of a few trees.

The dark aura skirted along the edge of the fairway, just out of sight from the plush green ranges of the golf course. It appeared that Dacey's murderer kept to the thin strip of woods edging the golf course.

"Shit. Back up," Dacey whispered, her voice urgent as they started to emerge. She nudged Gideon back into the woods, hiding them from view. She gave the large white building a wary look but sighed in relief when no one seemed to notice them. "Don't let anyone see you. This is a private military golf course. We're going to stick out like sore thumbs here."

Gideon looked at Dacey in her oversized borrowed clothes, flip flops, and straw hat, and then down at his work jeans and faded t-shirt and had to agree.

The tranquility of the scene, combined with the picturesque surroundings, offered a momentary respite from the shock of the bloody crime scene they'd just left behind. Gideon couldn't help but appreciate the serenity of the green plains, contrasting with the shadowy woods.

The golf course was an oasis of calm and quiet. Foot traffic was minimal, merely consisting of a few individuals clad in polo shirts and crisp khakis who were more interested in their game than the world around them. The only sounds piercing the quiet being the occasional rhythmic thunk of a golf club making contact with a ball and the distant cawing of seagulls gliding overhead. The scene seemed to exist in a bubble of its own, untouched by the chaos and murder that occurred in the woods only a few hundred feet away. Gideon watched as two men strode across the parking lot and disappeared inside the cool interior of the pro shop. To the side of the building, a plethora of golf carts lined up in neat rows, each one primed and ready for a golfer.

As Gideon took in the sight, the bright sunshine cast a golden hue over the landscape, accentuating the lush greenness of the golf course's grass. The well-manicured fairways stretched out to their right, inviting golfers to play.

Gideon looked over to Dacey, ready for her guidance. "What do you sense now?" she asked.

He closed his eyes against the bright morning sun. He tilted his head back and forth, feeling like a bat sending out echoloca-tion. "There," he said, opening his eyes and pointing to a parking spot only a few feet away. "The trail ends there."

"Come on," Dacey murmured, sidling over towards the spot. Keeping her body mostly hidden from the pro shop by the bushes, she looked around the area.

Gideon stayed out of the way and kept watch as Dacey bent down to examine the pavement. She looked up from her examination of the asphalt, shaking her head. "Yep, this is the spot. Look – you can see a little bit of blood here. Either this wasn't his first rodeo, or he had supplies like a tarp or something, but there is way less blood than expected. If that's the case, it means this was premeditated."

"You think he planned to kill you?"

"Not me specifically. But he was planning to kill someone last night. I just happened to fit his M.O." Dacey stood up, dusting off her hands on her pants. "He must've put us in a car and taken us to a secondary location. This is a dead end for now. I need to review the reports from last night – see if I can find something to give us direction."

"What if that doesn't turn up anything?"

"Then we'll give the responding officer and the coroner a visit."

Gideon's phone ringing interrupted his next question. Pulling his phone out of his pocket, he cringed at the name on the display screen.

"Shit. I didn't realize how late it's already getting," Gideon murmured under his breath. He pressed the phone to his ear. "Hey, Ma."

"Where are you? Is everything okay?"

"Yeah, Ma, everything's fine. I just got hung up with some work stuff and am running behind. I should have called and let you know."

Dacey shuffled closer, looking curious as Gideon talked to his mother.

His mom huffed an exasperated breath. "Would you please let me know when you're going to be late? Will you be heading home soon? I have stuff for breakfast ready to go and I don't want it to go to waste."

"Not this morning. I'm helping a friend for a little bit before I head to the shell shack. Please enjoy your breakfast without me. And I'm sorry I forgot to call you."

"I'm hungry. I could eat," Dacey's voice piped up from next to him.

"Who was that?" his mom's suddenly eager voice asked in his ear as he gave Dacey an aggravated look.

"That's just my friend Dacey, Mom. Don't worry about breakfast. I'll see you later after my shift."

Gideon tried to end the call, but his mother interrupted him. "Nonsense. Bring her over, Giddy. We have plenty of food. I'll make pancakes!"

And then, in a total mom power move, she hung up the call before he could formulate any additional counterarguments. He gave Dacey a flat look for inviting herself to breakfast. She didn't understand what she had just unleashed. She gave him an unrepentant grin.

Gideon's mom's ever-hopeful, ever-romantic heart would take one look at Dacey and pin all her hopes for his bleak romantic future on the tough-as-nails bennu shifter. Then, later over dinner, he would have to field a slew of questions he wouldn't be able to answer. If he didn't get ahead of this, his mom would be fantasizing over whether her future grandbabies should call her Nana or Meemaw. And then he'd need to break his mom's heart by making sure she understood that there was zero chance of anything romantic ever happening between him and Dacey. Not that it would probably even make a dent in her undaunted enthusiasm.

With a resigned sigh, Gideon shrugged; whatever happened with his mom, it would play out however it did. He'd deal with the fallout when the time came.

"We should go. I don't want to make her wait too long."

CHAPTER 9

They followed their previous path back the way they came, an oppressive heat filling the woods. The usual cooling breeze off the Gulf of Mexico was blocked by the trees, making sweat start to drip down Gideon's back. He glanced over and enviously realized that Dacey seemed unaffected by rising temperatures.

The entangled vegetation seemed to close in, wrapping them in a shroud of silence. The only noise was the chirp of crickets and the rustling of their passage through the foliage. After emerging back onto the sidewalk, they quickly made their way back to Gideon's car.

Gideon caught Dacey staring at her phone in apprehension. "What's wrong?"

Dacey blew out a slow breath. "I need to call Isabel and I am dreading it."

It took Gideon a moment, but then he remembered where he'd heard the name before. "Is that George's wife or a family member?"

"Wife," Dacey confirmed. "Well, shit. I can't put this off any longer."

"Do you think it would be better for someone to do that in person?"

"Normally, I'd say yes. But I don't have the time to head back home. And I know Isabel would rather have me focus on finding George's killer."

Rolling her shoulders, Dacey pressed the call button and brought up the phone to her ear. Gideon could hear the ringing and then a soft feminine voice greeting Dacey. He suddenly wished he was anywhere else but in this car.

"Hey, Isabel. I have bad news—"

The woman must've heard something in Dacey's voice because she was crying before Dacey could even get an explanation out.

Gideon drove, sitting in excruciating silence as Dacey calmed the sobbing woman down and told her what happened. He glanced over at Dacey, wincing at the drained, heartbroken look on her face.

The apartment Gideon shared with his mom was almost halfway between Gulf Breeze and Niceville, so it wasn't long before Gideon was turning off his car and giving the front door to his apartment an apprehensive stare. Dacey was still on the phone with Isabel, consoling her and vowing to make whoever killed George pay.

After finishing the call, Dacey leaned back in her seat, rubbing her eyes vigorously with her knuckles. Gideon watched as she packed away her emotions. After all the therapy Gideon had been through, he was very familiar with compartmentalization. Dacey closed her eyes, leaning back in the passenger seat, and took slow, measured breaths. The deep line between her brows smoothed out, and the white-knuckled grip she had on her phone slowly eased. She opened her eyes and turned to Gideon. He would have thought she was perfectly fine if it wasn't for the blazing fire burning in her irises.

"I could use some pancakes," Dacey confided, making Gideon snort out an inappropriate laugh.

"Well, then, let's get you some."

They didn't even make it to the front door before it was flung open. Gideon's heart skipped a beat as his mom popped out of the entrance like a whack-a-mole. With a wide smile on her face, she beckoned them inside, her excitement palpable. Gideon's apprehension grew as he watched his mom practically glow with happiness. Gideon didn't really have any friends in Gulf Breeze – the few people his age in town were living a bohemian beach life-style. In contrast, Gideon was so busy with two jobs that he was mostly living a paycheck-to-paycheck lifestyle, which didn't lend itself to rum runners and fish tacos at the tiki bar on Fridays.

"Mom, this is my friend Dacey Menet." The pause on the word 'friend' was barely perceptible. His mom gave Dacey such a heartbreakingly hopeful look that his stomach curdled. "Dacey, this is my mom Stella Bean."

"Mrs. Bean, it's so nice to meet you," Dacey said with a smile. "Thank you for opening your home to me."

"Oh, please. Call me Stella."

Gideon barely managed to keep from staring at Dacey incredulously. Who was this sweet, warm, friendly woman?

And he almost groaned out loud when he realized that Dacey was still wearing his borrowed clothes. Based on the glee in his mom's eyes, she was clearly spinning tales. Gideon could almost hear the wedding bells ringing inside her mind. She waved them both towards the kitchen, leading them to the old diner table they had acquired when Betty's Diner had permanently closed its doors.

As Gideon stepped into the kitchen, his feet glued themselves to the floor.

Oh god. His mom had pulled out all the stops.

She had covered their scruffy table with her special holidays-only tablecloth, topping it with her best plates. She'd even pulled out the fancy store-brand paper napkins instead of using paper towels as usual. A vase sat at the center, showcasing a couple of blooms that bore an uncanny resemblance to the ones adorning the oleander bushes near the entrance of their apartment complex.

Gideon couldn't help but feel a mix of embarrassment and pride at his mom's enthusiasm, knowing that she had gone to great lengths to create a warm and welcoming atmosphere for their meal.

"Sit, sit," his mom commanded, waving them to take their seats.

"Let me help, Ma," Gideon countered. "I'll get the drinks."

He gave the contents of the fridge a quick peek and set the jug of orange juice on the table. "We've also got water or coffee. You want any?"

"Yes, coffee, please!" Dacey requested, pouring herself a glass of juice. "I need some caffeine in the worst way. Oh, with cream and sugar, please, if you have it."

Gideon's mom deposited bacon, an enormous stack of pancakes, and scrambled eggs onto the table. She looked around the spread, checking to see if she'd forgotten anything.

She snapped her fingers, making a tsk-ing sound. "Almost forgot the salsa. Can't eat eggs without it," she confided to Dacey.

"Yes!" Dacey cheered. "I'm the same way."

"Really? Giddy thinks I'm weird. He doesn't get it."

Gideon wrinkled his nose at them. "Tomatoes are disgusting."

Stella threw her hands up. "And yet you love ketchup! How can you hate tomatoes but like ketchup?"

Gideon fell back on his oft-stated argument. "They're completely different. Besides, it's the texture of tomatoes that's the problem, not so much the taste."

Dacey and Stella giggled, apparently bonding over Gideon's dislike of gross, mushy tomatoes.

The morning sunlight filtered through the windows, casting a warm glow upon the scene. Plates were piled high with food. As Gideon's mom set a bowl of salsa on the table, Dacey's eyes lit up with delight.

"I'm starving. Everything looks so good. Thank you for cooking for us, Stella."

Stella gave Dacey a pleased grin. "I love cooking, but it's usually just the two of us, so it's not worth making a big spread. Mind if I say grace real quick, Dacey?" Stella asked, the deferential tone catching Gideon off guard. Normally, his mother was all about 'mother knows best', not 'mother asks permission'.

"Not at all, Stella," Dacey replied, her dark eyes sparkling with an unfathomable emotion.

With a nod of thanks, Stella closed her eyes, bowing her head slightly. "Thank you, God, for the food on our table and friends, new and old. Amen," she murmured, her lips curling into a warm smile as she opened her eyes.

Conversation flowed easily as they indulged in their meal, sharing stories and laughter. Gideon couldn't help but be amazed by the sheer amount of food Dacey consumed. The sight left him momentarily speechless, his own fork hovering mid-air.

"Gideon's never mentioned you before, Dacey," Stella piped up, giving Gideon a pointed look. "Tell me, how did you two meet?"

The fork making its way to his mouth wobbled, dangerously close to losing its cargo. Gideon couldn't believe he didn't think to come up with a cover story before they showed up.

"We met through my work," Dacey replied smoothly.

"Oh? At the shell shop?"

"Sorta. I'm a private investigator. I had to come into the shell shop when I was on a case, got to talking to Gideon, and we hit it off."

"Oh wow! A private investigator! That sounds so exciting," Stella cooed. Gideon could already imagine how his mom must be weaving fantastical tales of car chases and stakeouts.

"It can be. But mostly, it's sitting around with a camera or filing paperwork."

"And Gideon is helping you on a case?" Stella asked.

Inspiration struck Gideon. "Not really, Ma. Dacey's car broke down early this morning, and she just needed a ride. Her clothes got ruined while she worked on her engine, so I lent her some spare stuff I had stored at the crematorium. I'm just going to be chauffeuring Dacey around until her car gets out of the shop."

Gideon knew that his mom was hoping for something juicier, but this would allow him to have a ready explanation as to what he and Dacey were doing together. And it would allow him to smoothly have an excuse when Dacey inevitably moved on with her life, and they never saw her again. He really didn't like lying to his mom, but he needed to protect her from the mess he'd found himself in.

"Say, Gideon," Stella began gently, laying down her fork and turning to face him with raised eyebrows, "you planning to come along to church with me this Sunday? It's been a while, hasn't it?"

"Uh…" Gideon hesitated, glancing at the clock before letting out a small sigh. He'd known this conversation was coming; it was almost routine now, as predictable as the seasons changing. "I have work, mom. The shell shack really needs me to cover Sundays; it's one of their busiest days."

Stella's face fell slightly, but she pressed on. "I think it'd be good for you, dear," she pushed gently. "Community's important. And maybe it'll take your mind off… things."

Gideon hesitated, knowing she was referring to his ongoing struggles with his mental health. But he was careful not to give away his deeper hesitation about attending her church. The judgmental glances, the sermons that more often preached about hellfire and brimstone rather than uplifting messages… it was all a little too intense for his taste.

But Stella continued, brightening her previous disappointing news, "What about you, Dacey? I'm sure everyone at church would love to meet you. And I promise, the pastor's sermon is always enlightening."

Dacey blinked in surprise, but quickly recovered her composure. She gave a charming smile, inclining her head. "I appreciate the offer, Stella," she replied graciously, glancing briefly at Gideon before looking back at his mother, "but I'll have to take a rain check for this Sunday."

"Of course, dear," she replied, her disappointment fading just enough to look back at Gideon, "Just thought I'd ask. Now, would you like some more coffee, Dacey?"

Gideon's gaze drifted to Dacey and noticed her coffee cup was empty. Knowing how his mom felt about how guests should be treated in their home, he pried himself from his comfortable sitting position and ambled toward the counter where the coffee pot was situated.

Behind him, a burst of heat and light filled the room so fast and sudden that Gideon spun around, coffee pot forgotten in his hand.

Dacey at the table with her fiery wings spread out in a blaze of ethereal light. It was a sight to behold, the way they flickered and danced like a flame. But before he could even voice his surprise, the wings dissipated, extinguished as if they never existed. The room fell back into the comfortable darkness, the afterimage of her wings burned into Gideon's retinas.

Had Dacey lost her damn mind?!

Dacey only glanced up from her plate momentarily, giving Gideon a nonchalant look. "You okay?"

Her words shook him from his momentary shock. Gideon's mouth gaped open, but no words came out. What was he supposed to say? He wanted to shout at her for igniting an open flame in his mom's house but looking around, he could see that nothing was on fire or singed. It was barely any warmer in the room than it was before Dacey unveiled her wings. He glanced over at his mom, but she was busy spooning heaps of salsa on her eggs and seemed to have missed the weirdness. She glanced up at Dacey's question, looking at Gideon worriedly.

"Yep, I'm fine," Gideon finally replied. "Just stubbed my toe. Here, Dacey, let me refill your mug."

Trying to appear unrattled, Gideon walked over to the table and poured Dacey a new cup of coffee before checking his mom's mug. His breath hitched subtly as he tilted the pot, topping it off to the brim. The coffee splashed into her cup, disturbing the thick surface of creamer, and swirling into a light mahogany. He then deposited the coffee pot back to its warmer, the glass surface clinking as it returned to its resting place. The scent of rich coffee permeating throughout the room was comforting, a subtle reassurance of normalcy.

Gideon retook his seat at the table, ignoring his mother's concerned glances. He knew he was acting like a jolty robot, but he found it impossible to get his nerves completely back under his control after Dacey's little stunt. He forked up a bite of egg, projecting an air of 'this is totally normal, everything is normal' with herculean effort. Stella gave him one last worried look before turning back to her plate.

A few minutes later, Stella exclaimed in surprise.

"Oh, shoot! The time got away from me. I've been having such a nice time getting to know you, Dacey. But I've got to get on the road; I need to open the shop."

Stella stood up and started to gather some of the dirty dishes. Gideon waved her away. "Don't worry about the dishes, Ma. I'll take care of it."

Stella gave him a hesitant look. "You sure? I know you need to get to work soon as well."

"I have plenty of time before I need to head to work." Gideon turned to Dacey. "Mom works at the hardware store – practically runs that entire place."

"Oh, stop! I'm just the cashier," Stella scolded, her cheeks blushing fiercely. Gideon got his complexion from his mother, and they both were world-champion blushers.

"Mom, you're selling yourself short. You organize all the shift schedules and manage all the deliveries and the inventory. You know where every single item in that store is located. Whenever there is an issue, everyone knows to come to you, not the owner. Hell, Mr. Donovan hardly needs to come in because he knows you'll take care of everything. I really think you should ask to be promoted to manager. That place would fall apart without you, and he knows it. I'm sure he'd give you that raise – he can't risk losing you."

Stella waved him off, blushing again and mumbling something about not being qualified. Gideon was frustrated but didn't want to argue with his mom again.

CHAPTER 10

Gideon watched out the front window as his mother's car drove away before pinning Dacey with a hard stare. "Care to explain why you almost gave me a heart attack and unleashed your fire wings inside my mom's kitchen? She worries about me already, so making me flip out in the middle of breakfast is not helping."

Dacey appeared entirely unperturbed in the face of Gideon's anger. "Being an auramancer is hereditary. I wanted to check if your mom had the ability."

"You thought the solution to that was to bust out your wings of fire over pancakes and bacon? What if she had been an auramancer? How would scaring the shit out of her help? She cooked you breakfast!"

"Oh," Dacey murmured, looking a little sheepish. "Yeah. I didn't think that through. I just thought she might be in denial like you were."

Gideon sputtered. He was so outraged that words failed him.

Dacey shrugged. "Well, she's not an auramancer. So, no harm, no foul. That means you probably got the ability from your father."

Gideon decided he'd had enough. He rubbed his temples, trying to relieve the pressure growing there. He needed to get away from Dacey and take a moment to come to terms with his new, altered reality. She had pulled him so quickly into her fantastical world of magic, murder, and mayhem that Gideon had found himself unexpectedly in the deep end without a floatation device.

He turned and started gathering the plates and cutlery with jerky movements. Filling the sink with hot, soapy water, Gideon started washing the dishes. He spoke over his shoulder, not turning his attention away from the task at hand.

"Best of luck, Dacey, but I can't help you anymore. As soon as I finish the dishes, I will drop you off wherever you need to go next. You said you have a local hotel room so I can also take you there. But I need to get to work. I can't let my mom down."

"Gideon, come on, man. Don't. Seriously, I need your help." Gideon stared at Dacey incredulously, gritting his teeth in frustration. She gave him a pleading look. "I never beg, but please. I don't have a ride. Plus, I lost my handler last night. I need some backup. I'll cut you in on the take."

"You didn't 'lose' your handler. He was murdered while working with you. I am not qualified to help. I will probably end up in a cardboard box like George. I don't know what I'm doing. I'm not trained and will most likely just get in the way."

"You're already doing great. There's nothing to train for. You just need to accompany me and help me identify magic. Easy peasy."

"Easy peasy? That's a lot easier to say when you can't be killed, but some of us aren't so lucky."

"I mean if someone killed me and then buried me instead of setting me on fire, it's basically the same as killing me."

Gideon gave her an unimpressed look, then rolled his eyes and turned back to the dishes.

Dacey paced behind him, twisting her fingers together. Once

he put the last of the now-clean dishes in the rack to dry, he turned back, leaning against the counter to watch Dacey pace. When she finally paused mid-stride, he gave his watch a pointed look, letting her know that she was running out of time. Her gaze locked with his, the ring of fire around her pupil flaring brightly for a moment. There was a resolute determination in her eyes that made him second-guess his reservations.

"Gideon," she said firmly, "I understand your worries, but you're the only one who can help me. Your unique ability to sense and identify magical auras is invaluable. I might be at a dead end, and you are the only person who can recognize this guy's aura. I need your ability to track down this killer before he murders more people."

Gideon turned back from the dishes and leaned his hip against the counter as he considered Dacey's plea. Biting his lip, he shook his head. "I'm not risking my life for this. My mom needs me."

Dacey gave the kitchen a calculating look before turning her gaze back to Gideon. "I'll cut you in on half my fee if you help me. You look like you could use it."

Gideon opened his mouth to refuse again when Dacey interrupted him and told him the amount he'd receive if he helped. Gideon closed his mouth so quickly that his teeth clacked.

"I can do this without you. But I really want your help. Look how much you've already assisted. Come on, let's find the killer before he strikes again. Please...."

Gideon sighed, realizing the truth in her words. It was true that his heightened sensitivity to magical energies had proven useful earlier that morning, even if he still doubted his own capabilities. Dacey's unwavering faith in him was both comforting and unsettling at the same time.

Gideon sighed in resignation. "You could give my mom a run for the money in the guilt department."

"Does that mean you'll help me?" When she gave him a sweet,

hopeful smile, Gideon knew he was done for. He was a sucker. And a dumb one at that.

Reluctantly, he nodded, his resolve growing now that he'd made the decision. "Alright, Dacey. I'll help you. But promise me we'll prioritize safety and caution. I don't want either of us getting hurt."

Dacey raised her fingers to her forehead in a salute. "We'll be careful, scout's promise. We're totally going to solve this. And I can help you work with your magic."

Gideon decided against mentioning that she'd used the wrong fingers for the scout's promise. If she'd ever been a scout, he'd eat his shoe.

$\mathcal{D}$acey let out an exasperated sigh as she tossed the coroner's reports onto the back seat. "Ugh, these reports are making me car sick. I'm about to puke up my pancakes," she grumbled, rubbing her temples. "I hate reading in moving vehicles. I'll just have to review them at the hotel."

Gideon glanced at her with concern, his grip on the steering wheel steady. "We'll be there soon."

"Your mom is awesome, by the way."

A warm smile tugged at the corners of Gideon's lips. "Yeah, she's the best. She worked her ass off to keep a roof over our heads. It's always been just the two of us against the world."

Dacey nodded. "Sounds like you guys were lucky to have each other. She's pretty, too."

Gideon chuckled, his cheeks slightly flushed. "Oh, I know. You should've seen how my high school buddies would flock to my house after school, finding excuses to hang around so they could talk to her. They were always making comments about her being a MILF. Back then, it used to drive me crazy, but I'm used to it now."

Dacey couldn't help but laugh at his lighthearted response.

"Well, your mom rocks. I'm glad I got the chance to meet her. And she makes a mean pancake."

"I noticed that you liked them. How many did you eat anyway?" Gideon teased.

"Honestly, I would've eaten more if it wouldn't have raised eyebrows. Regenerating always leaves me starving. Being reborn burns a ton of calories."

Gideon stared out the window as they passed Sheryl's Shell Shack. He'd called out sick before they'd left his house and headed towards Dacey's beachside hotel. His boss had been irate when Gideon told him he was too sick to work but settled down when Gideon pointed out that he never called out sick and often covered other people's shifts.

"So, if it's just you and your mom – what happened to your father?"

"I'm the product of a one-night stand. My mom had been out with some of her college friends celebrating after finishing their finals, and she drank a little too much. She never got the guy's number or even his last name, so when she found out she was pregnant, she couldn't track him down."

"That must have been hard for both of you," Dacey remarked softly.

Gideon's grip on the steering wheel tightened, his gaze fixed ahead. "Yeah, sometimes it was tough. My grandparents were traditional and conservative. When they found out she was pregnant without being married, they kicked her out of the house. She had to drop out of college to support us. But she never let that get her down. She was an amazing mom. It wasn't until I hit my teens that I started to realize just how much she sacrificed for me."

Silence filled the car momentarily, broken only by the sound of the passing traffic.

"Do you ever wonder about your father?"

Gideon let out a sigh, his eyes glancing briefly at Dacey

before returning to the road. "Not really. I mean, I've thought about him from time to time, especially when I believed I was hallucinating and going crazy. But honestly, what would I even say to the guy now? We've built our life without him. We didn't need him then, and honestly, we don't need him now. He was just some dude who donated some DNA, as far as I'm concerned."

"If we figure out who your father is, he's going to have a lot of explaining to do. My bosses are going to be pissed."

"What? Why?" Gideon asked, his brow wrinkling in confusion.

"Think about it. This guy almost certainly knew that he had magic and had a one-night stand with an uninformed human. He left you both unprotected, Gideon. It's… unethical – at best – to be so careless." Dacey sighed, her gaze intense. "You were an infant with magical abilities and no warning or training. You couldn't protect yourself. Your life, and your mother's, were put at risk."

Gideon looked at her in disbelief. "Unethical? I didn't ask for any of this, Dacey. I'm trying to figure it out just as much as you are," he responded defensively, his voice growing louder.

"That's not it, Gideon. You're missing the point. It's not about blaming you… it's about responsibility. Unprotected magic is dangerous. It's the kind of thing that puts everyone in danger of discovery. Us, the Mythicals. I mean… you thought you were crazy because you had no idea what you were dealing with and no idea what you are."

The silence that followed was deep, broken only by the car's engine and the gentle roar of the ocean to their right.

"So… what do you suggest we do?" Gideon asked quietly.

Dacey returned his gaze, determined. "We start by cleaning up this mess, Gideon," she said, her voice resolute. "Once we complete the investigation, you should think about finding out who your father is. Even if it's just to punch him in the nose for being so stupid and thoughtless. Oh, that's my hotel just up ahead."

Gideon looked where Dacey was pointing and spotted a hotel painted in tones of peach and seafoam green. It looked like something straight out of corporate America's guide to seaside design: an ordinary stucco, steel, and glass structure that someone had taken a casual wave brush to in the hopes of transforming it into a relaxing beach retreat. The pink-and-teal nautical theme that drenched the hotel was as blaring and unapologetic as a sunburn.

From the off-center sailboat logo that adorned the hotel's façade to the seashell motifs embedded into the concrete driveway, the entire venue screamed, 'beach-inspired'.

At Dacey's directions, Gideon parked the car in the spacious parking lot that was only half-filled– it was off season for most tourists. Stepping out, Gideon stopped and enjoyed feeling the salty breeze on his face.

Walking inside the hotel felt like entering a maritime time capsule, replete with tacky ocean-inspired decor – framed paintings of seagulls in flight and waves crashing upon the shore, table lamps shaped as seashells, and concierge staff in Hawaiian shirts, their acrylic nametags sparkling under the fluorescent lights. It was as though someone had siphoned all the soul from a true beachfront property and funneled it into this sanitized, corporate interpretation.

And yet, there was something undeniably charming about the effort – like a child trying to recreate their favorite beach vacation with a shoebox diorama. The potted palm trees scattered across the lobby, white wicker furniture covered in bright floral cushions, and old crab traps repurposed to be side tables. The wispy net curtains hanging from every window evoked the image of breezy beach cabanas.

Instead of heading toward the elevator as Gideon had expected, Dacey approached the front desk. "I'm expecting a package," she stated to the bored front desk attendant behind the service counter.

The attendant managed to pull on a semblance of interest and inquired, "Name and room number?" without looking up.

"Dacey Menet, 417," she replied, maintaining a business-like tone. The clerk knelt behind the counter before pulling out a large, bland-looking cardboard box, the size of roll-on luggage. Groaning under the weight of it, she placed it on the desk with a thunk, eyebrows lifting in surprise and curiosity.

Gideon, watching this unfold from a distance, was quick to step forward. "Allow me," he offered politely, ready to adopt the role of a gentleman, before taking hold of the surprisingly hefty parcel.

He followed Dacey to the elevator, pretending like his arms weren't straining under the weight. Once inside her tiny suite, Dacey pulled some clothes out of an open suitcase, stating her need for a shower as Gideon gently set the box on a table.

As she disappeared into the bathroom, he took a moment to look around the room, taking in the coastal decor. The real draw for the room was the small balcony with a view of the beach and the bright water of the Gulf of Mexico.

Gideon found himself rooted by the large sliding glass door leading out to the balcony, his gaze magnetized to the sight outside. Even though he'd spent almost his entire life living near the beach, the beauty of the Gulf of Mexico still occasionally caught him by surprise. The sun had clambered its way up the sky, showering the wind-swept beach in a radiant, golden glow that made the blue-green water sparkle like diamonds. His eyes traced the silhouettes of people dotting the sand, exploiting the heat for pleasure while he was mired in a mystery. His fingers grazed the cool windowpane, a silent spectator of a world he craved but seemed far beyond his reach.

Gideon heard the water turn on for the shower and realized that Dacey had left the door to the bathroom cracked open. He was undecided if she trusted him or was unconcerned if he posed a threat. He had a feeling he knew which it was but shrugged it off. A suitcase sat open on the floor; inside was a haphazard pile of clothes in dark colors. Nothing that looked like it belonged in a beach town.

Gideon couldn't help but wonder where Dacey called home. He turned his back against the ocean, leaning against the glass, and called out to her over the sound of running water, "So, Dacey, where do you live? Are you nearby?" He kept his question casual, keeping all hints of hope out of his voice. In his thoughts, he was already trying to figure out how to see her again. Even just as a friend. She was the first person in a long time who didn't look at him like he was weird, or broken, or scary.

Through the steam-filled bathroom, Dacey's voice floated back to him, her tone muffled but audible. "I live in Tallahassee," she replied.

Gideon's heart skipped a beat at the idea. Although it wasn't exactly in his neighborhood, it was only a few hours' drive away. The idea of having a connection, even if it required a bit of travel, ignited a flicker of excitement within him. He imagined the possibility of future encounters and the adventures they could share.

"But I also have a small studio apartment in Savannah," she continued, "where the local Conclave is located. For work, I sometimes have to spend extended time at HQ."

Must be nice to be able to afford two places, Gideon thought with no small amount of envy.

A moment after the water turned off, Dacey emerged from the bathroom, dressed in jeans and a dark button-up shirt, towel-drying her wet hair. When she barely spared him a glance as she stuffed her feet into a pair of boots, Gideon realized he was being almost as unrealistic as his mom about the potential for any kind of relationship with Dacey.

He couldn't help but ask, "What's a conclave?"

Dacey paused, a thoughtful expression crossing her face. "A Conclave is essentially a committee of magical beings," she explained. "It's kinda like a secret society that oversees the well-being and activities of Mythicals in their area."

"Are you part of the Conclave?" Gideon asked.

"I'm not a member of the main council. I fall under the umbrella of the Savannah Conclave, and I usually work for them, but they'll lend my services to other Conclaves if they need my help. They're kind of like a government entity, but they're pretty hands-off from the internal politics of the local Mythical families, packs, and clans." Gideon listened intently, his fascination growing with each word. He never imagined that there could be a hidden world operating alongside the human realm. It gave him a glimpse into the depth and complexity of the supernatural world, one that he was only beginning to understand.

"I'm only called in when someone is doing something that might expose the existence of Mythicals," Dacey continued. "My specialty is tracking down Mythical murderers – especially serial killers. We can't risk exposure – we'll either be annihilated or sent to labs to be experimented on. Compared to humans, there is just not enough of us to fight back."

Gideon's admiration for her deepened. She was responsible for keeping an entire species safe. It seemed like a lot of responsibility on her shoulders.

"Here," Dacey said, interrupting his thoughts when she slapped a folder against his chest. "Look over these reports and let me know if you see anything odd."

CHAPTER 12

$\mathcal{D}$acey looked up from her police report. "Do you know this Officer Kaminski or Dr. Leroux? Have you ever met either of these guys? Either of these men ever come into the crematorium?"

Gideon shook his head. "I've seen the name Dr. Leroux a bunch. Whenever I do a cremation, I have to check the death certificate against the permit form, so I see that name all the time. But I've never actually met him. And I don't know Kaminski. We don't get the police reports at the crematorium. And I try to keep away from the police. After the whole fiasco in college…"

Dacey nodded. "I can imagine." She glanced back at the cremation document in her hand that she was comparing to the police report she'd been emailed. "Yeah, both of these guys have some questions to answer. Kaminski and Leroux have been doing some creative writing here. It says that George's body was found in his hotel room after having a heart attack. Neither report mentions the GSW at all. I need to call operations."

Gideon watched out of the corner of his eye as Dacey made her call, his attention dropping from the report he was supposed to be deciphering. As the phone rang, she tapped her foot impatiently.

"Hey, Wiz," Dacey spoke into the phone, her voice strident. Curiosity gnawed at Gideon as he wondered who Wiz was and how they could help. He couldn't help but try to eavesdrop on Dacey's conversation. "We've got a bigger situation brewing in Gulf Breeze than I anticipated. Something isn't right. I think we need to send in a team to contain this. How soon do you think you can get everyone here? Really? Well, shit. I'll just hold down the fort until then. Hey, did you get a look at my death certificate? Apparently, I'm fond of heroin. News to me! And did you see George's paperwork? Yeah, a heart attack. Unless the bullet wound in his chest caused cardiac arrest, it's all bullshit. The coroner and at least one police officer are involved in something shady. Can you have Leonhard check and see if he can figure out if either one is a Mythical? If anyone could figure it out, it'd be the Numerai. I need to know if I'm dealing with humans or something else. Also, we need to send someone to retrieve George's body asap." Dacey paused, cutting her eyes over to Gideon and meeting his stare. "Yeah, he's still with me. And, yes, he's definitely a Mythical of some kind. I'm almost certain he's an auramancer... Gideon Bean, 7120 Navarre Parkway, apartment 312. Good idea. Hold on and let me find out."

Dacey turned the phone away from her mouth and turned to face Gideon, not noticing his incredulous anger. "The Wiz wants your email address and phone number."

He raised his eyebrows at her, shocked by her presumption. "You gave them my home address without asking me if that was okay. I don't appreciate it."

Rolling her eyes, Dacey told the person on the other line to hold on. Pressing the phone to her chest so they wouldn't be overheard, she gave him a look like she thought he was being ridiculous. "Of course, I did, dude. You are a Mythical. And a rare one, at that. They're going to want to know who you are. The

Conclaves were established to protect our people. They can't protect you – or protect the rest of the world from you – if they don't know you exist. Now, the Wiz wants your email address so she can send you some information about what being an aura-mancer means. So how 'bout you pull up your big-boy pants and conduct your freak out later when you're alone and won't get on my nerves."

"Stop calling me dude."

"Okay, Giddy. I'll stop calling you dude," Dacey snarked. Gideon gritted his teeth. Only his mom was allowed to call him Giddy.

He gave her a flat look. "Thanks, Candy. I appreciate it."

Gideon knew he'd hit a direct shot when Dacey sucked her front teeth, her expression very annoyed. He could hear a feminine voice laughing uproariously despite the phone's speaker being pressed to Dacey's chest. Deciding not to push her further, Gideon rattled off his email address and phone number.

Without further comment, Dacey pulled the phone back to her ear. "You get that? Okay, good… I don't care." Dacey rolled her eyes. "He can't be your new favorite recruit – he doesn't work for the organization. You haven't even talked to him yet… You know what? Fine, he's your favorite. Can you just get me the home addresses for both the cop and coroner? Perfect. I need to go."

The next ten minutes were spent in awkward, aggravated silence, both reading their respective reports and ignoring the other. Dacey blew out a relieved breath when her phone dinged, alerting her to an incoming message.

"The Wiz got us the info. It looks like the doctor lives closer than the cop. We should head there first."

Gideon handed Dacey the reports he was reading as she got up from where she'd been lounging on the bed. "The Wiz? Is that like a name or a title?"

"Neither. Her real name is Octavia. But everyone calls her the

Wiz because she's a wizard and because she's a whiz on the computer. People have been calling her the Wiz for so long that half the team doesn't even know her real name anymore."

Dacey opened the sealed box that had been waiting for her at the front desk when they'd arrived at the hotel. Gideon could feel his eyebrows crawling their way up to his hairline as Dacey rummaged through the box, grabbing weapons of various shapes and sizes. She strapped them securely to different parts of her body with practiced precision. Her movements were swift and confident. Gideon got the impression that she could accomplish the task with her eyes closed.

She tossed an empty duffle bag to Gideon, which he caught against his chest and stared at in befuddlement. Before he could question her, she held out a lighter and a small bottle of accelerant.

"Are we planning to burn down the doctor's house?" he asked.

"No. I don't need matches for that," Dacey raised her hand and waved her fingers. Each of the five digits had tiny flames burning from the tips of her fingers like birthday candles. With a final flick of her fingers, the flames all extinguished. "Um, this is for you in case I get killed."

At Gideon's darkening expression, Dacey held up placating hands. "Listen, this is vital. If something happens to me, your number one priority is to get me somewhere secluded and set me on fire. The accelerant will help speed up the process, but I'm flammable, so all you really need is a lighter or a match. It's the only way to bring me back. Also, make sure you stand back. When I regenerate, I do so with a bang."

Her gaze met his, thinking that Dacey was pulling his chain, but her eyes were dead serious. Gideon hesitated but then dipped his head in acquiescence. He dropped the accelerant into the bag and stuffed the zippo into his pocket.

"This is a pretty big bag for just two items," Gideon murmured absently.

"Oh, that's so you can stuff my body inside. You don't want to get caught lugging my corpse around. That kind of thing tends to end with an arrest."

Words failed Gideon at her nonchalance at the prospect of dying and being set on fire. He stuttered, trying to come up with some sort of pithy response but, in the end, just dropped his shoulders and accepted that while he was with Dacey, weird and strange were the new normal.

When Dacey tried to hand Gideon a gun, he shook his head, mumbling something about not knowing how to use it.

A look of incredulity crossed Dacey's face, her eyebrows furrowing. "Didn't you grow up in the South? How is it possible that you don't know how to use a gun?"

"This is Florida. It's not really the South."

"Um, excuse me. You live smack dab in the middle of the Redneck Riviera. This is northern Florida. Everyone knows that in Florida, the more north you go, the more southern you get."

Gideon couldn't help but sputter out a laugh.

CHAPTER 13

"Shit," Dacey grumbled from the passenger seat, giving the elegant gates barring them from the doctor's neighborhood a dark look.

She fished her phone out of her pocket and dialed a number. After a moment, Gideon could hear a man's voice through the speaker. "Hey, Dace, I assume you're calling about the police officer and the coroner... They are both human, unless I'm mistaken. And I'm never mistaken. So, you got anything else for me? I'm bored senseless. The encryption they have me breaking on the Sullivan case is too easy."

"You live for that shit, Leonhard; don't lie to me," Dacey teased. "I've got a couple of things I need. Last night, around 11 o'clock, I was at the Ruby Tuesday restaurant, and then I walked east down John Sims Parkway. Can you see if you can get access to any surveillance videos along my route? I'm hoping we can get eyes on the perp. The second and more immediate thing I need is to get into a fancy gated community. The neighborhood is called Coral Isle in Destin, Florida. Do you think you can get into the system? Also, the owner of the house we're heading to is named Dr. Claude Leroux. You're certain he's human?"

The voice scoffed. "I'm a Numerai. Yes, I'm certain. Coral Isle, you said? Unless it's a closed system – and there's no way it is – I can get into it. Give me five minutes."

"One more thing," Dacey gave Gideon a look that made him tense up. "I want you to open a file on a Professor Blackwood. Hold on… What school, and when did he attack that student?" Dacey asked Gideon.

"University of North Florida. About six years ago," Gideon responded.

"Do you happen to remember the name of the woman he attacked?" When Gideon shook his head, Dacey shrugged. "No worries. She's not the fish we're gonna fry anyway."

"Will anyone really do anything about it after all this time?"

Dacey's eyebrows raised, and she clucked her tongue. "Oh yes, we take this kind of shit very seriously. The guy was so sloppy that he left a witness. If there's a rogue vampire operating in my neck of the woods, I'm going to take that very personally."

"I'll look into him and see if any red flags come up," Leonhard replied. Gideon could hear the rapid staccato clicking of a keyboard as the man hung up without another word.

"Let's pull around the corner and out of sight so we don't arouse any suspicions. The last thing we need is some nosey neighbor noticing us hanging around and calling the police."

Making a quick U-turn, Gideon spotted a doctor's office that overlooked the entrance to Coral Isle. Finding a spot that had a little bit of shade, he parked the car and turned to face Dacey. With a curious expression, he asked, "So, that Leonhard guy said that he's a Numerai? What's that?"

Dacey leaned back in her seat, steepling her fingers under her chin like she was a lecturer imparting important knowledge. It made Gideon want to cross his eyes and stick his tongue at her. "They are Mythicals with an innate connection to numerical patterns, calculations, and mathematical concepts. They possess an inborn ability to see patterns and decipher the mysteries of numbers and symbols. Leonhard told me that he's descended from André-Marie Ampère. There isn't a computer system that Leonhard can't hack. He can complete complex mathematical equations easier than breathing. He's created all these systems to monitor news, police reports, markets, internet rumors, and more – all just to ensure that Mythicals won't get outed. And he said that was just a side project for when he gets bored. It was his system that alerted us to something strange happening here."

Gideon's interest grew. He had always been intrigued by the fantastical and the unknown – he grew up on Harry Potter just like everyone else his age. The thought of a creature with such incredible abilities fascinated him. Dacey continued, "Numerai are said to be rare and reclusive, often dwelling in hidden sanctuaries deep within forests or secluded fortresses. They guard their knowledge fiercely and are highly sought after by those who wish to uncover hidden secrets. That's the legend. My experience has only been with Leonhard, who is an uber-nerd that will talk computers and math for days on end and pretty much lives in a man cave. Don't bring up artificial intelligence unless you need to cure insomnia."

Gideon pondered the implications of having a Numerai on speed dial like Dacey did. The idea of having access to someone with the ability to crack any system seemed both exhilarating and daunting. Gideon was aware that if he possessed such abilities, he'd probably exploit them for financial gain. Could he be trusted not to try and get into a bank vault, given the opportunity? Certainly not. He'd be able to pay rent for a year.

With each new crumb about the Mythical world, Gideon felt a growing determination to delve deeper into the realm of myths and magical creatures.

Gideon and Dacey sat in the car, their eyes fixed on the grand entrance gates of the doctor's exclusive neighborhood. He watched with a tiny amount of envy as the occasional sleek, high-end vehicle glided through the wrought-iron gates, disappearing into the luxurious community beyond.

Just as another elegant car approached the entrance, Dacey's phone buzzed. She quickly glanced at the screen and smiled, her excitement palpable. "Got it," she exclaimed, relaying the gate code to Gideon. They waited for the other car to disappear around a bend, before driving up to the key box. With slightly trembling fingers, he input the code Dacey recited.

As the gates buzzed and slowly began to open, Gideon let out a breath he hadn't realized he was holding, relieved that no siren or alarm had sounded. Pulling through the gate, he gave his car a chagrined look. The hatchback stood out like a turd among diamonds. Hopefully, if anyone saw them, the assumption would be that they were hired help.

Gideon guided the car forward, driving along the winding streets lined with majestic palm trees. The streets were meticulously manicured, exuding an air of elegance and privilege. The weight of their mission pressed upon him, but he remained resolute, knowing that their presence in this prestigious neighborhood was necessary to uncover the truth.

As they cruised along the palm tree-lined avenues, Gideon let out a low whistle as he scanned the grand houses, searching for the specific address they sought. The sheer magnificence of the neighborhood left him momentarily awestruck as he marveled at the affluence and extravagance that surrounded them.

Dacey seemed unimpressed with their surroundings. She had her nose stuck in her phone and barely glanced up from the screen to take in the neighborhood. "What are you doing over there?" Gideon finally asked.

"Leonhard sent us a quick rundown on this guy. His information says that Leroux is unmarried. He's forty-six and originally from Louisiana. He moved here six years ago from Baton Rouge. He drives a white Range Rover. According to his Facebook profile, he's an avid golfer – a member of the Indian Bayou Country Club. Fancy schmancy."

"Well, at least we won't have to worry about dealing with a wife."

Dacey nodded distractedly, still reading up on their target.

"That's it," Gideon announced, pointing towards a mansion that was slightly smaller than its neighbors. It was a Mediterranean-style two-story house adorned with a terracotta tiled roof and stucco siding. Large windows filled the front of the house, framed with wrought iron accents. On the second floor, balconies and terraces were enclosed by ornate railings. Gideon could imagine having a cocktail in one of the many lounge chairs while enjoying a gentle breeze and panoramic view. Like its neighbors, the mansion sported a lush green lawn, palm trees, and painstakingly landscaped gardens.

"Pretty nice place for a coroner," Dacey commented drolly.

"What's the plan now that we're here?"

Dacey leaned over the back of her seat and retrieved her floppy straw hat and sunglasses and put them on. Gideon gave them a doubtful look, thinking that the cheap vacation wear clashed with the neighborhood. This was not the kind of place that tourists would accidentally stumble into. "We're going to pretend that we are visiting family but accidentally mixed up the house numbers. Pull into the drive. I want you to open your senses as we approach and tell me what you feel."

"What if he recognizes you?"

Dacey scoffed. "People don't expect the dead to resurrect, so their brains can't make that connection. A corpse looks a lot different than when they're alive. Plus, coroners see so many bodies that they stop paying attention to what the people look like after a while."

Gideon didn't know how he felt about the fact that it sounded like Dacey had died often enough to have that kind of knowledge.

Pushing away the morbid thought, Gideon pulled into the winding driveway that led to the grand mansion. The pristine drive was lined with lush greenery and vibrant flowers as it guided them around a small fountain nestled in the center of a circular drive. Gideon stopped the car and parked it near the front door, ensuring a quick escape if needed. The imposing presence of the mansion loomed before them as they stepped out of the vehicle, their footsteps echoing softly on the brick-paved path.

Approaching an enormous set of etched-glass French doors, Gideon glanced around, trying to see if anyone had noticed them yet.

"You picking up anything?" Dacey murmured, barely moving her lips.

Closing his eyes momentarily, he focused his senses, allowing his intuition to guide him. At first, all he could sense was the heat of Dacey's magic. With some effort, Gideon muted Dacey's aura so he could focus on the rest of the environment around them.

There it was – the trace of that same dark magic emanating from around the mansion. But as soon as he tried to grab onto it, it slipped through his fingers, dissipating into the air. When Gideon turned his focus on the house itself, it was as if there was nothing there. It was like there was a void taking up the space where the mansion sat.

His eyes popped open, and he looked over at Dacey, nodding. "I think so, but I'm not completely sure. There is a very faint feeling of it, but so weak that it's almost non-existent. I'm not sure if that counts. It feels like the assailant who attacked you, but I'm having a hard time holding on to it. It keeps slipping away when I focus on it."

"Do you think he's home?"

Gideon shook his head. "Maybe, but I'm not certain. I don't feel anything coming from inside the house. It's like a blank slate.

Maybe I'm picking something up from the backyard or a neighbor?"

"The house is a blank slate? That's weird. You don't feel anything from the house at all?" When Gideon shook his head, Dacey gave the mansion a suspicious look. "If we're assuming that it's Leroux's magic that you are sensing, you should be picking up something more from his house than a trace of an aura if he spends any amount of time there. Leonhard said that Leroux is human and he's usually not wrong about that kind of thing. Normal humans don't give off a dark magical aura. Perhaps you're picking up someone with magic that has only visited and doesn't live here."

Gideon shrugged as they made their slow way up to the front door, as mystified as Dacey over what he was sensing as she was.

As they stood before the grand entrance, with the heat of the day at their back, the massive doors gave Gideon pause. He tried to peek through the glass to see into the house, but the translucent doors only left him with the impression of a tiled entryway filled with space and light. A few blurred shapes of walls and furniture further inside were all he could see past the foyer. The only sound was the soft splashing from the water fountain behind them.

With a deep breath, Gideon reached out and pressed the doorbell, the metal cool beneath his fingertips. Standing in the shade of the front door's alcove, the chime resonated through the quiet air.

"Someone's coming," he whispered to Dacey when he saw a subtle movement behind the door.

Out of the corner of his eyes, Gideon watched as Dacey rolled her shoulders as if she was adjusting an ill-fitting jacket. Worried that something was wrong, he turned in Dacey's direction, and was taken aback by the eager, happy smile on her face. If she noticed Gideon's shock, she didn't react as she kept her attention on the door. She looked like an entirely different person, as if she was possessed by the spirit of a peppy sorority girl.

Before he could ponder her transformation further, the door swung open, revealing an older woman dressed in a uniform with gentle gray hair styled in a neat bun.

A swell of dark, malevolent magic washed over Gideon so thickly that he felt like he was choking on it. He couldn't even speak to warn Dacey. Gideon stumbled back and turned his back to the maid, pressing his hand firmly over his mouth to keep from vomiting.

Thankfully, Dacey seemed unaffected as she smiled warmly at the women. Thinking quickly, now that the worst of the sensation had passed, Gideon pretended to sneeze. The woman softly said, "Bless you", as Gideon turned back towards the entrance, schooling his features into a placid expression. Thanking the woman, Gideon took minute slow breaths through his nose, trying to get his gorge completely under control.

Dacey's voice broke the awkward moment, her tone polite yet purposeful. "Good afternoon. We're here to see Dr. Leroux. Is he available?"

Her words hung in the air, and the maid's eyes flickered with a hint of something that Gideon couldn't identify. A moment of silence passed, allowing a palpable tension to settle between them. Gideon studied the maid's features, noting the subtle lines etched on her face, but he wasn't sure if they were the result of age or stress.

The maid's voice, calm but guarded, finally responded. "I'm afraid the doctor is currently not home. May I inquire about the nature of your visit?" Gideon finally got his stomach under control and shifting closer to Dacey on the stoop, he kept his expression calm and friendly.

Dacey took a single step slowly closer to the maid, her face earnest and hopeful, but stopped when the woman gripped the door in a tight hand. "I'm Cynthia, and this is Patrick. We're members of the Dolphin Conservation Alliance. One of our members, Alan Kaminski, who is also a friend of Dr. Leroux's, said that he was interested in learning more about our initiative. We'd love to speak with the doctor if he is available."

A flash of impatience washed over the woman's face for a split second before it was wiped away and replaced with a bland professional smile. "I'm sorry. Doctor Leroux is not home. If you'd like to leave any pamphlets, I can make sure he receives them."

Gideon would bet his whole paycheck that if they gave her any pamphlets, they'd immediately find their way into a garbage can.

"Can you let us know when you expect him home?"

The woman was shaking her head before Dacey even finished voicing the question.

"I can't give out that kind of information. If you'll excuse me, I need to get back to work."

The woman started to close the door when Dacey stepped in the way of the closing door. "Did I get my schedule wrong? I thought he was supposed to be home today – or is he out golfing? Kaminski mentioned that he's an avid golfer. I think they were meeting at the Indian Bayou Country Club. Wait – or was it the Eglin golf course? Man, I need some caffeine, I've got all our client's schedules mixed up."

The maid's lips tightened, and her professional smile started to look a little strained around the edges. "I'm sorry, I still can't give you that kind of information. If you don't have any pamphlets to give me, then I really must insist you go now."

"Of course!" Dacey chirped. "I'm so sorry to interrupt your day. Thank you for your help."

The woman's face softened slightly. She dipped her chin in acknowledgment and then closed the door, leaving Gideon and Dacey standing alone in the shade of the front porch's overhang.

"What the hell was that?" Gideon muttered, finally able to

breathe properly now that the door was closed again, and the dark magic was shuttered.

"What?" Dacey asked, tugging him away from the front door and back towards his car.

"The moment the door opened, awful dark magic poured out. I could barely breathe."

"Really? Someone must've warded the house. I can't believe I didn't think of that." Dacey gave him a pleased look. "So, tell me what you sensed."

"It was kinda similar to the magic trail of your murderer. Although… slightly different. Maybe it was just stronger. My senses were completely overwhelmed." Gideon wanted to dust off his clothes because he felt like the corrupted aura was still clinging to him. He tried to explain the sensation to Dacey but wasn't sure he had the words to convey the feeling the aura left.

When she asked if the person with magic had been home, but hiding from them, Gideon shook his head. "I have no idea. It was really overpowering, so maybe?"

Dacey turned and stared at the house for a long moment before making a sound of frustration. Muttering under her breath, she started to walk back to the car, waving Gideon to join her. "Well, that was a bust," Gideon complained.

"Not entirely. As far as I can tell, the maid didn't know the name Kaminski. If she'd ever heard of him, she would have had a reaction – even a small one – at the mention of his name. She also had a small reaction to Eglin golf course, so she's heard the name before. It's a military-owned golf course. I need to have Wiz check and see if it gives memberships to non-military people."

"Eglin? Like the one we were at this morning?"

"Yep," Dacey responded, popping the 'p' sound. "Somehow, I don't think that's just a coincidence that it's the same place I was taken last night."

"Where to now? Do you want to go to the golf course?"

Dacey pursed her lips as she thought over their next step. "Not yet. Pull out and park down the street, out of line of sight from the house but where we'll see anyone coming or going. The maid was lying about something to us – I'm just hoping it's about whether Leroux was home."

CHAPTER 14

Gideon slid uncomfortably into the driver's seat as Dacey got into the passenger side of the car. The leather stuck to his skin as the suffocating heat of the car wrapped around them, even though they'd only been gone a few minutes. The air inside the vehicle was stale, like a long-abandoned attic, and it clung to his lungs uncomfortably. Ignoring the sweat pricking at his forehead, he cranked on the AC, turning it to its highest setting. His callused hand nudged the window control, letting in a sliver of the morning's breeze, eagerly anticipating the relief that would eventually cascade into the vehicle.

Gideon guided the car along the driveway, glancing back and forth between the windshield and the mansion in the rearview mirror. Though outwardly identical to neighboring Florida McMansions, its nondescript facade caused a shiver to worm its way through Gideon, slithering its insidious way down his spine. He swallowed hard and forced himself to pay attention to the almost non-existent traffic in the luxurious neighborhood as he cautiously pulled the car out onto the road.

A few houses down, Gideon switched the gear once more and parked the car on the street beneath the meager shade of a tall palm tree. The car shuddered to a halt, the engine sputtering a final cough before settling down. Gideon resisted the urge to pet his car's dash, internally praying that it wouldn't leave them high and dry.

Gideon and Dacey adjusted their mirrors to capture the perfect view of the house behind them while also scanning for oncoming vehicles. Gideon tried to keep his attention parked on the view in his rearview mirror.

There was something unnatural about the silence that hung bloated and expectant around them; a silence that was almost as unsettling as the house they were spying on.

He glanced sidelong at Dacey and found her with brows furrowed deeply. He saw the fringes of anticipation curling in her fiery gaze, like a telltale spark of a bird of prey waiting to strike. Beside him, Dacey shifted restively, lost in thought as she tapped a fingernail on her thigh.

No longer able to stand the silence, Gideon asked, "So, is this what your… job is usually like?" He gestured vaguely to the quiet neighborhood outside the car.

Dacey snorted. "Yeah, it's not as action-packed as last night would make you think," she rejoined. "If it was like that all the time, I might actually enjoy it more." She ran a tanned hand through her dark curls, a few sparks danced around her fingers like rambunctious fireflies. Gideon wondered if Dacey knew that she threw off invisible sparks when she was agitated. "Most of it is as boring as watching paint dry."

Just as Gideon opened his mouth to ask her to elaborate, she started explaining.

"You'd think dealing with magical beings would be full of glamour and excitement, right? But the reality is, even the most supernatural of creatures still need to do their grocery shopping and pick up their dry cleaning." She leaned back in her chair, a far-off look in her eyes as she pondered on her statement. "It's more like being a private investigator. I spend hours in cars tailing suspects, magically inclined or not, watching them go about their terribly ordinary lives."

"Really? That's…" Gideon trailed off, clearly surprised at the admission.

"Boring?" Dacey finished for him, chuckling as Gideon nodded sheepishly. "Yeah, it's not all it's cracked up to be. You wouldn't believe how often being a Mythical is just as boring as a regular human – even the murderous ones."

Gideon nodded slowly. He had always assumed that the supernatural world, if it existed, was full of constant excitement and danger. But to hear that, in many ways, it was as mundane as his everyday life? It was disconcerting and reassuring in equal measure.

Gideon stole a glance at her; his own unease momentarily stilled at the sight of the fire-touched woman showing any sign of annoyance. A tease was on the tip of his tongue when her strangled noise snapped his attention back.

"Hey, you alright?" Gideon immediately asked. Her dark gaze was fixed on the car's side mirror, her hands clenching around the edge of her seat. Her earlier boredom was forgotten, replaced with a sort of electric excitement. Following her intent stare, Gideon squinted through the rearview mirror at the heat-hazed street behind them.

"Look! A white Range Rover. That's got to be him. I knew that maid was lying to us. He was home!"

Gideon saw just in time a shiny white Range Rover slipping out from Leroux's driveway. Among the Teslas and the Bentleys lining the pristine streets, the Range Rover blended seamlessly; it wouldn't have even been noticeable in the high-end neighbor-hood had they not been vigilantly watching for it.

Gideon slid down low in his seat, attempting to become inconspicuous as the sleek Range Rover cruised past their stationary car. He squinted, trying to glimpse through the dark tint of the high-end vehicle's windows, but the Rover's impenetrable darkness revealed nothing. The SUV glided past, leaving Gideon craning his neck and a silent question hanging in the air.

A ripple of excitement, thrilling and unfamiliar, bubbled up Gideon's throat. It rolled around inside him, simmering beneath the veneer of his usual composure. He'd never fancied himself much of a thrill-seeker, but the uniqueness of his current companion lent everything an air of surreal intrigue. He realized that he was having fun.

"Follow that car. I've always wanted to say that," Dacey instructed, her voice full of the same excitement that filled Gideon. The words were classic and cliché, reminiscent of old spy movies. But they filled Gideon with a bubbling thrill.

Carefully, to avoid drawing attention, he urged his old hatchback to life, the engine sputtering in a protest that had become its norm – he really couldn't afford a trip to the mechanic. Gideon adjusted his rear-view mirror back to normal, and slowly pulled out behind Leroux. His heart thundered, a staccato rhythm against his rib cage, as he glanced at Dacey.

"Don't get too close, right?" she instructed. "Keep it inconspicuous. Once we get onto the main road, try to keep a few cars between us and Leroux."

Gideon gave a curt nod, settling back into his seat and making himself loosen the white-knuckled grip he had on the steering wheel. "Right," he agreed.

As the Range Rover pulled through the gates to exit the Coral Isle community, Gideon waited a few beats before following.

Gideon spotted Leroux's vehicle up ahead, its shiny white exterior reflecting the brilliant sun overhead as it turned east onto the I-98. The surroundings slowly changed from gated communities to quickie marts and grocery stores.

"He's turning," Dacey announced urgently, pointing to where the SUV was pulling into the turn lane at a stop light. Cursing under his breath about jerk drivers who don't use their turn signals, Gideon also pulled into the turn lane with one car between them and Leroux.

"Do you know where this road leads?" Dacey asked, pointing to the street sign that said SR 293.

Gideon shrugged. "State Road 293?" indicating the two-lane highway that stretched off into the distance. "It leads to the Mid-Bay Bridge, which will take us back to Niceville."

Recognition flickered in Dacey's eyes.

"And other than that," Gideon continued, resting his hand on the frame of the window, "there's not much else down the road. Just a few residential neighborhoods, a middle school, and such."

"Interesting that he's headed back to Niceville. I doubt that it's just a coincidence. Kaminski lives in Niceville... maybe he's visiting him? Or perhaps he's headed to the coroner's office."

Gideon shook his head. "I doubt it. The coroner's office is in Pensacola. If he's headed there, he's taking the scenic route. It's way faster to take 98 west to get to Pensacola. If he circles up through Niceville, he'll add like an hour to his commute."

Gideon's gaze locked on the back of Leroux's gleaming Range Rover, its taillights a bright splash of red against the bright sky-blue day. Between them and Leroux, another car waited at the turn light obliviously.

And then, with a casual flippancy that had them both cursing, Leroux shot through the traffic light, the Range Rover taking an illegal left turn between a break in oncoming traffic. Gideon's grip on the wheel tightened, the vehicle beneath him thrumming with shared impatience. But the driver ahead remained blissfully ignorant and stationary. Hamstrung by driving laws, they could only watch as their quarry slipped further away. Each second, as the traffic light gleamed red, was a fist tightening around Gideon's heart. Gideon briefly considered whipping around the car ahead of them but figured that drawing that kind of attention to themselves would thwart the whole purpose of stalking Leroux.

When the light finally turned green, a change that seemed to have taken an eternity but was probably less than a minute, Gideon hit the gas, the car surging forward with a grumbling roar. Dacey tensed beside him, her eyes focused ahead.

Gideon swerved onto the main road, feeling like a stock car racer as he wove through the traffic, a needle threading through the two-lane road's tapestry of lights and cars. He kept his eyes peeled as they tried to locate Leroux.

"Do you see him?" Gideon asked as he quickly passed a slow-moving truck.

There was a beat of silence before Dacey exclaimed, "There! Look! Up ahead on the right!" Gideon followed her pointing finger and spotted the familiar Range Rover way up ahead.

It was a dangerous dance, the rhythm of the town's traffic and their desperate chase. Gideon was acutely aware of Dacey's gaze focused ahead, acting as another pair of eyes as they followed the trail of the once again visible Range Rover.

A large square metal building painted in shades of blue appearing up on the right caused Gideon to curse and clench his jaw.

"What?" Dacey demanded.

"That's the marina," Gideon said, indicating the building as he switched lanes again and gunned the engine as fast as he felt safe doing. "We're almost to the bridge, which means this road is about to merge down to one lane."

Dacey shot him a quick, dry smile. "Okay, just do your best not to lose him, Gideon."

Right as they came abreast of the marina, the road merged down to one lane. Gideon huffed out a breath, wishing they could have gotten closer. "It could be worse," Gideon conceded. "We're only three cars back."

Up ahead the Choctawhatchee Bay opened before them, a wide expanse of sparkling water interrupted only by the bridge bisecting it. To their right, the marina hugged the shore, where boats of varied sizes dozed peacefully within their assigned berths. A few masts pointed at the cloudless sky, resembling sentinels guarding the other sleeping vessels. The rippling water reflected bright wavering lights on the hulls of the boats, playfully distorting their sleek shapes.

Ahead, barely a few feet off the water, was the Mid-Bay Bridge. The concrete structure hovered close over the green-brown waters, except at the center, where it rose into a majestic arch, allowing for the passage of gliding boats underneath the traffic.

The greenish-gray-brown waters of the Choctawhatchee Bay bore a stark contrast to the gorgeous blue-green of the Gulf of Mexico. But it was still pretty with small white caps on the choppy water reflecting the bright sunlight making the water sparkle like a diamond-encrusted swath of fabric.

Once they left the bridge behind, the surrounding landscape transformed into untamed and undeveloped Florida cypress scrub forest. There was a welcome tranquility to the highway, a solitude in its undulating lanes which were bordered by an endless expanse of ragged undergrowth and spindly cypress trees. Gideon slowed the vehicle and fell back, allowing a chasm to grow between Leroux's car and his own. The highway was almost deserted now, speckled intermittently with other vehicles. The last thing they wanted was for Leroux to realize he had a tail.

They went all the way to Niceville. He knew these ribbons of asphalt roads intimately, so he felt like he could make the trip with his eyes closed once he was sure where Leroux was headed.

They passed the Honeybee Ice Cream Shop and then a familiar Ruby Tuesdays.

"Do you think he's—"

"Headed to the golf course?" Gideon finished. "Yep. Look, he's turning."

Gideon's heart pounded uncomfortably in his chest as a strange sense of deja vu washed over him while he observed the

Range Rover turn into the entrance of the golf course. His grip on the steering wheel tightened as he slowed the vehicle as they drove past the entrance drive. In his periphery, he watched Dacey. Her fiery eyes were glued to the scene unfolding in front of them.

Leroux casually leaned out of his car's window to converse with the entrance attendant inside the gate booth. Gideon could see little more than the sight of Leroux's receding hairline. His angular face was turned away, obscured by shadows and distance and sunglasses.

"Shit! Damn! Keep going. Don't follow him," Dacey exclaimed. They exchanged a glance, their expressions mirroring a shared understanding. There was no way that Leroux wouldn't notice his POS car pull in behind him to the fancy golf course.

"We can't just follow Leroux into Eglin without giving away our game," Dacey said. "I don't want him to know that we're on to him. The cockroaches will scatter before we've flushed them out." In response, Gideon gave a resolute nod, turning his attention back to the street before them.

Once they were almost a block past Eglin, Gideon spared a glance at Dacey, concerned over her silence. She was gnawing on a thumbnail, looking lost in thought.

"What now?" Gideon asked, pulling Dacey from wherever her thoughts had taken her.

"I think Officer Kaminski's house is nearby. Why don't we stop by and see what we can scope out? Leonhard's info says that he works the early morning shift, so he's going to be out."

CHAPTER 15

$\mathcal{A}$lan Kaminski's house was in the middle of a quiet, oak-lined street.

Gideon parked the car under the shade of a magnolia tree overhanging the road, the engine sputtering to a stop. He stifled a yawn as his eyes fell upon Kaminski's modest, middle-class house. It wore the unmistakable stamp of being built in the 1980s, with sand-colored bricks and sun-worn wooden paneling adorning its exterior. It was the kind of house he would've given his left foot for as a kid – the kind of house where he imagined Saturday morning cartoons and microwaved hot pockets were the norm.

The vacant carport seemed to confirm that no one was home. Gideon and Dacey exchanged glances before getting out of the car. The sweet vanilla fragrance of magnolia blooms filled Gideon's nose as he glanced up and down the street, relieved to see no one appeared to be outside. It made sense; it was approaching the hottest part of the day.

"Same routine as before?" Gideon confirmed as they walked up the sidewalk past the baked, dying grass of the front lawn.

He cast out his senses as they approached the front door. The paint on the doorframe was slightly faded and cracked, revealing the passage of time. The scraggly and overgrown garden, mostly filled with weeds, by the entrance offered a glimpse of the home-owners' apathy or perhaps busy schedule.

The neighborhood itself, though nothing like Leroux's ostentatious one, possessed a comforting charm. Most of the houses were well-tended and from the same era. Gideon and Dacey stood before the modest house, pretending to check the address.

Gideon cut his eyes to Dacey. "I'm picking up another similar magical signature, but it's very faint."

"Curiouser and curiouser," Dacey murmured. "You picking up anything else?"

When Gideon shook his head, Dacey turned and knocked on the door. They waited a few minutes and knocked again. "No one's home." She cast a quick glance around, giving the houses in the neighborhood a sweeping look. With a subtle nod, she gestured toward a gate nestled within the tall wooden fence that shielded the backyard from any potential prying eyes.

Before Gideon could voice the argument that they'd probably get caught for very little reward, Dacey turned and scurried toward the gate.

Gideon cursed under his breath and quickly went after her, looking around in paranoia for onlookers. As Dacey slipped through the gate, he scanned the surroundings for any signs of neighbors or activity. Thankfully the street was still quiet and deserted. Gideon, feeling a surge of annoyance, muttered darkly under his breath before begrudgingly squeezing himself through the narrow opening.

Inside the backyard, a hushed stillness engulfed them, punctuated only by the occasional chirp of a lonely cricket. Sweat from both the heat and his overwrought nerves gathered in the small of Gideon's back. The temperature was oppressive, and they weren't even to the wretched heat of high summer yet. Florida only had four seasons: hot, not quite as hot, two weeks of almost cold, and rainy hurricane season.

Dacey moved cautiously, her steps calculated and light. Gideon, his heart pounding in his chest, tried to match her stealth but couldn't help but stumble over an abandoned shovel hidden in the overgrown grass. His frustration grew – at Dacey, at the situation, at his own incompetence, at his growing exhaustion that was making him clumsy.

Dacey, seemingly unfazed by his misstep, continued onward, her eyes scanning the area for any signs of whatever she was hoping to find. The backyard, probably once neatly landscaped, now bore further signs of neglect. Overgrown bushes tangled with each other, and a dilapidated shed stood in one corner, some rusted tools leaning carelessly against its outer wall.

Gideon's unease grew with every passing moment. He was worried that someone had witnessed them sneaking into a police officer's backyard and that they would be hearing the wail of approaching sirens at any minute. But as he glanced at Dacey's determined expression, he knew that retreating was not an option unless he planned on abandoning her.

Dacey paused by a battered picnic table, its wooden surface gray and splintered, worn down by time and weather. Along the back wall, abandoned pots and a few scattered gardening tools sat haphazardly against the siding. The pots contained the remnants of dead plants, withered and shriveled.

Breaking the silence she turned to Gideon, her voice a hushed whisper. "Do you sense any magic coming from the house?" He hesitated for a moment, trying to attune his mind to the subtle currents of energy that flowed around them. "Just a little," he responded uncertainly. "It's faint, similar to what I felt at the doctor's house."

Dacey's eyes sparkled, the fire within them glowing and burning. "Place your hand on the window," she suggested, curious and confident. "If your magic is strong enough – and I think it is –

with practice, you'll be able to 'see' through wards and other magical defenses."

Gideon hesitated, his hand hovering uncertainly in the air before finally pressing against the cool glass. As his palm made contact, a jolt of energy coursed through him, tingling with sparking intensity. With a curse, Gideon snatched his hand off the glass, shaking it out and then checking it for injury.

"What happened?" Dacey asked.

"It felt like I got zapped. Like static electricity but worse." Gideon rubbed his hand on his thigh, trying to disperse the lingering irritation. Looking at his palm, it was redder than usual – although that may have been from wiping it on his jeans – but that was the only sign of the shock.

"That was the ward. I'm amazed you can feel it. That probably means you have strong magic. It's a good thing – with practice, you're gonna be able to do some cool stuff." Gideon wanted to ask more about this 'cool stuff', but Dacey turned back to the house again. "You should try again. Just don't try to push physically past the ward, only psychically. Kaminski might have set up the ward to signal him when its border gets crossed."

Taking a fortifying breath, Gideon let it out as he slowly pressed his palm back against the glass. He gritted his teeth against the shock, but now that he was ready for it, it wasn't so bad.

The glass warmed under his palm as he closed his eyes and tried to sense what was beyond the windowpane. "So, I can push my senses past the ward, and it won't trigger the alarm?"

Dacey hummed. "Yes, I believe so. It should only be set to trigger when a physical presence breaches it. However, we should get ready to run if I'm wrong."

Deciding that her answer was good enough for him, Gideon closed his eyes and released his senses. They splashed up against the ward surrounding the house like waves against a sea wall. Centering himself with a deep breath, Gideon pushed them further. He expected them to pop through the ward like a needle through a balloon, but instead, they just seemed to permeate through slowly, like liquid seeping through dense cloth.

The essence of dark magic flickered at the edges of his perception. Pushing harder, he finally felt his magic slip fully into the house. Gideon's breath caught in his throat, shocked and overwhelmed by the rancor of the magic swamping his senses.

With each passing moment, Gideon's connection to the magic deepened, the barriers between the visible and the hidden thinning until they no longer existed.

Finally, Gideon yanked his hand away, not able to endure another moment. He turned to Dacey, but she must've seen the answer in his eyes because she gave him a smirk and asked, "Same magic, yeah?"

Gideon nodded. "Similar, not exactly the same."

"I have a theory, but we'll need to ask some experts about auramancer magic to confirm. I'll tell you in the car."

~

"What was your theory?" Gideon asked as he started the car and turned the A/C to blast air into his overheated face. "Why do these guys' magic feel similar but not completely the same?"

Dacey leaned back in her seat, rolling her shoulders. "I believe that what you're sensing is a related species of Mythical. See, there are often... I guess you'd call them sub-species within a 'genus' of Mythical beings. For example, there are different types of shifters, all with their own unique magical aura. If you met them, they'd all have shifter magic but would feel slightly different depending on the sub-species. So, a badger would feel slightly different from a fox, and a fox would feel different from a bear."

Gideon listened intently, absorbing her words. He felt like if he could just meet more types of Mythicals, he'd be able to better understand his magic ability. Maybe he could even find out what type of monster emitted the magical aura that he detected at Kaminski's house. He couldn't help but feel a surge of determination to uncover the truth hidden within the realm of Mythicals.

"How many species of shifter are there?"

"Oh man, I don't even know… Hundreds, maybe more?"

"Really? That's amazing. Do you know many shifters?"

"My landlord is a jaguar shifter. I know a few others, but I know her best."

Gideon's next question got stuck in his throat at the thought of hundreds of types of shifters existing in the world without anyone's knowledge.

CHAPTER 16

"So, where are we headed next?"

Dacey blew out a breath, looking heavenward as if that held the answer to his question. "I guess back to my car. I'm so tired that I'm starting to circle the drain. I need to call Wiz and Leonhard and have them dig deeper into our suspects. I want to find out how Kaminski and Leroux know each other. And I want to see if they have any connection to anyone else at Eglin. You can get some sleep, go into work tonight like usual, and then I'm hoping we'll have something to work with by tomorrow."

Gideon started to nod, feeling exhausted himself, but then froze. "Wait a minute. You told me this morning that you needed my help because you didn't have a ride. Now you're asking me to drop you off at your car. What the hell, Dacey?"

Gideon suddenly remembered her grabbing a set of keys from the box on Mr. Peterson's desk and stuffing them into her pocket. She had keys to her car the entire time.

"I did need a ride. My car was abandoned when I got murdered. It might even be impounded by now."

He kept his eyes on the road, furrowing his brow in annoyance at Dacey's lie by omission. He couldn't believe she misled him. His grip on the steering wheel tightened, and he let out an exasperated growl.

Dacey, sitting beside him, maintained an unrepentant expression. When he glanced over at her, she met his gaze squarely and coolly explained, "No need to get your panties in a twist. I needed to ensure you came with me. Stopping these murders is important, Gideon."

His eyes narrowed, and he shook his head in disbelief. "I understand that your case is important. But I don't like being lied to."

She nodded, her expression solemn. "Alright, I understand. Seriously. I hear you, Gideon. It won't happen again."

Taking a deep breath to calm himself, Gideon refocused on the road before him.

He was so distracted by his irritation that he realized he was driving without direction. "Where's your car?"

Dacey glanced up from her phone, where she'd been busy typing. "Oh, yeah. My car is behind the Ruby Tuesday. I really hope it didn't get towed. That would be such a pain in the ass."

Less than fifteen minutes later, Gideon was pulling around the back of the restaurant. Dacey let out a relieved breath when she spotted a blue sedan among the smattering of other vehicles. Once she got out of his car, Dacey stopped and turned back, leaning back into the vehicle. "Hey, are you available tomorrow morning? I want to follow up with some of the victims' families and I'd like you to go with me."

"I'm scheduled to work the morning at the shell shack. I don't think I can call out two days in a row and keep my job. Could I help you after my shift? I will be done by 1."

"Yeah, I can work with that. Call me when you're ready, and we can start again. I'd really like your help. You're the only one who can identify the magic we're looking for. I'm hoping that Leonhard will have something useful for us by then." Dacey pulled her phone out of her pocket and handed it to Gideon. "Put in your number so I can call you if I need you."

Taking her phone, he input his number and sent himself a text. On his own phone, he saved her number under the name 'Candy', smiling to himself at the thought of how annoyed that would make her.

Then he drove off, watching in his rear-view mirror as Dacey got into her car.

Gideon shook his head at himself, rolling his eyes in exasperation towards his own burgeoning thrill at the prospect of tomorrow's possible adventures. He still held an inkling of distrust towards Dacey, even though he liked her fiery spirit and biting humor.

As Gideon turned his vehicle towards home, the long night and morning finally caught up with him. With eyelids as heavy as lead, every mile that passed under the wheels seemed like a Herculean task. It felt as if he were driving through mist, his senses swirling, and his focus threatened to fracture at every turn. The excitement and adrenaline that had kept him going drained away, leaving him feeling like a husk. He turned on the radio and sang along to a pop song to keep himself alert.

Once he pulled into his apartment complex, every step up to his front door was like trudging through molasses. The need for sleep accompanied every beat of his heart; his body felt like it was made of stone. He fumbled to unlock his front door, his fingers uncomfortably clumsy.

The world around him moved in slow motion as he stumbled his way through his house, kicking off his shoes haphazardly and dumping his wallet and keys on his dresser. He stripped down to his boxers, foregoing his usual bedtime routine. He barely had the energy to pull back the covers on his bed before he collapsed into it.

CHAPTER 17

The sun was just cresting the horizon, barely beginning
to lighten the sky as Gideon pulled into his usual
parking spot in front of his apartment. His shift at the crematorium had been particularly long that night – uneventful, but long
and boring, nonetheless. The sharp scent of formaldehyde that
always clogged up his nostrils felt like it was still clinging to his
clothes. He'd slid every corpse into the retort oven that night half
expecting them to come back to life. Seeing Dacey rise from the
flames had been haunting, but also exciting. The thought of her
stirred something foreign in his chest, an inkling of fascination,
and perhaps, an ounce of… He shook his head, trying to dislodge
any thoughts along that path.

Gideon had less than an hour before he needed to be at the
shell shack, and he felt like his stomach was trying to gnaw its
way out of his body in hunger. Although, if he knew his mom, he
knew to expect an interrogation served alongside his breakfast.

His entrance was announced by the familiar creak of the
wooden floorboard and the soft chime of dainty bells his mother
had hung on the door. The cushions on the worn-out couch in
their modest living room had seen better days. Yet the little space

was impeccably clean and had a comforting air about it, thanks to his mother.

As he walked into the kitchen, Gideon found his mom at the stove, deeply engrossed in preparing breakfast. "Morning, Ma," he greeted her. "You need any help?"

His mother, with her kind eyes and brown hair with a few gray strands pulled back in a ponytail, looked up. A warm smile found its way onto her face. "Good morning, love. Did you have a good night?" she asked, but her eyes remained worried. He knew that she didn't like that he worked at the crematorium.

"Yeah, it was a good night. Uneventful."

Unlike the night before, Gideon thought with a wry twist of his lips. His thoughts were interrupted by his mother's next question. "Will your new friend Dacey be joining us?" she asked. His heart stuttered at the mention of the bennu shifter.

"Not today, Ma," he offered nonchalantly, fearing his mother might see through his transparent emotions.

"Will we be seeing more of her?"

Gideon huffed a sigh, knowing exactly where his mother was going with her line of questioning.

"Probably not. Dacey lives in Tallahassee. Once she finishes her assignment here, she'll be going home."

"Are you two—"

"No, Mom," Gideon interrupted before she could finish the question. "We are just friends. I barely know her."

"Well, if she's still in town on Sunday, you should bring her to church. It would be a good way for you two to get to know one another better."

He shifted uncomfortably in his chair, staring unseeingly into his mug of coffee. One corner of his mouth twisted in a half-smile, half-wince. "Mom, y'know, I'm sure she would appreciate the invite – if she's even still in town on Sunday, but..." he started. Internally, he juggled his words with delicate precision, trying to find the most non-offensive way to decline her invitation to the Gospel Covenant Church. "But," he continued, "she's here to do a job and I don't think she'll have time to sit through a sermon."

His mother's eyebrows dipped as she stared at Gideon, disappointed. Gideon could see an inkling of her hurt feelings mixed with confusion. Gideon tried to respect her beliefs, but his mother just couldn't seem to understand and accept that he didn't want to go to church with her anymore. The church felt like a physical manifestation of the inherent tension between them. Yet, neither of them put these feelings into words. They rested on a silent standoff – her hope that he'd come to church and his desire to never step through its doors again. He hated disappointing her. However, he hated the idea of Dacey and him having to sit through a sermon preaching about fire and brimstone and damnation even more.

He dipped his chin once, locking eyes with his mother. He implored her mentally to understand, to not get upset. His mother held his gaze, searching his face as if she could extract the hidden truths in his features. She gave a slow nod before releasing a tired sigh, "Alright, kiddo," was all she said.

Once they finished breakfast in awkward silence, Gideon and his mom left the apartment together, and both headed toward their respective workplaces.

Gideon had begun working at Sheryl's Shell Shack when he was a freshman in high school. He'd thought he'd left the tourist trap behind when he went to college, but when he'd come crawling home, the manager Jared had given him back his part-time job with, if not welcoming, at least indifferent arms. As long as Gideon did his job without complaint, Jared was happy to just stay in his office and ignore the happenings inside the shop. In all the years he'd worked there, Gideon had never met the owner or even learned their name. All he knew for certain was that there was no 'Sheryl' for Sheryl's Shell Shack – it was just a catchy name, probably picked out by some anonymous marketing department in a corporate conglomerate.

The best thing about Sheryl's Shell Shack was that the shop's front wall was made up entirely of glass, offering an unobstructed view of the beach that was across the street from the shop – rolling sand dunes, seafoam froth kissing the shores, the cerulean vastness beyond.

Unlocking the front door, Gideon was immediately enveloped in an eclectic mix of smells distinctive to Sheryl's – the odor of cheap plastic, a hint of sugar from the saltwater taffy, and the brine of the nearby ocean, all overlaid with the smell of coconut oil from the aisle of suntan lotions. The shop was a clutter of beachside essentials – from foam boogie boards for the daring wave riders to an array of colorful and cheap t-shirts with silly slogans that often caught tourists' eyes.

A rotating rack that wobbled as it turned – showcasing stacks of picture postcards – stood alongside fridge magnets shaped like seahorses and starfish, jars filled with seashells displayed next to sunscreen and beach umbrellas. The scenery was all too familiar to Gideon, a comforting tableau of the ordinary, a place that spoke of sand, sun, and sea, of carefree laughter and summer flings, of life untouched by the peculiarities with which he suddenly found himself entwined. Given the time of year, Gideon didn't expect a busy day, giving him plenty of time to replay his day with Dacey repeatedly in his mind, overthinking every interaction. He suddenly wished it was already next month when the spring breakers would keep him busy his entire shift instead of giving him too much time to think about the enigma that was Dacey Menet and the revelation of his new 'powers.'

As a lonesome figure, Gideon navigated through the shop, turning on lights and prepping the store for the day's shoppers. Not long after unlocking the front door, the jangling of bells over the entrance woke him from his thoughts and brought him back to the present, announcing the arrival of a group of customers whose happy chatter disturbed the silence of the shop. A trio of elderly women, early risers, teetered in with determination and fixed eyes, scanning the assortment of knick-knacks lining the shelves.

One of the shoppers, a woman with peppery grey curls who was so thin she reminded Gideon of a walking skeleton being held together only by compression socks and determination, inquired about beach chairs. Forcing a welcoming, customer service smile onto his weary features, Gideon responded to their needs, helping the ladies carry their items to the register.

An hour into the day, after the trio had long ago trundled out of the door and their chatter had ceased, Jared sauntered in. Barely nodding an acknowledgment at Gideon, he made his slow, shuffling way to the back office. Based on the dark sunglasses he sported and the haggard look on his face, Gideon assumed he was hungover again. Gideon shrugged internally, returning his attention to the shop.

A middle-aged woman, her face flushed a bright pink shambled into the store next. Gideon gave her a sympathetic look and pointed her to the aisle with aloe vera creams and cooling gels when she asked about sunburn remedies. As he assisted her, the door jangled again, signaling another customer. Gideon looked over and recognized the tanned physique of a local – a surfer Gideon only knew by his nickname Zen, a moniker that Gideon assumed arose from his laid-back demeanor.

Raising a hand in greeting to Zen, Gideon started to say hello, but the words died in his throat, his hand frozen mid-air as something strange twisted his gut. An odd, flickering sensation emanated in the air from Zen, like the cool lapping of waves against Gideon's skin. As Gideon watched, aghast and fascinated, iridescent scales seemed to ghost across Zen's exposed flesh, their sheen dancing under the dim light. They formed strange patterns that moved and shifted, coloring Zen's skin in hues of opal and jade.

Gideon blinked, doubting his sanity. Staring unabashedly, his mind struggled to rationalize what his eyes perceived.

Zen, feeling Gideon's intense scrutiny, stopped in the entranceway and met his perplexed gaze. His brows dropped into a confused frown. When the lady he was escorting to the register stopped, realizing that Gideon was no longer at her side, he startled back into motion. His hand, still raised in an attempt at a greeting, was quickly pulled back in awkward defeat. Mortification bloomed in his chest as he called out a greeting to Zen.

"Good morning," Gideon called out, giving Zen what he hoped was a normal, friendly smile.

As Gideon bagged the woman's purchases, he kept one eye on Zen as the man picked out a block of surf wax. At first Gideon hoped that what he was seeing was a trick of the light, but Zen's skin still had a ghost sheen of iridescent fish scales.

What in the hell?

Once he finished the woman's transaction, Gideon turned his attention away from Zen and attempted to return to his duties, but he couldn't shake off what he saw.

Gideon schooled his face into a placid, neutral expression as Zen approached the register. Gideon's muscles were as rigid as steel beams and he couldn't stop his movements from being jerky with his growing nerves, the cold clatter of his anxiety echoing off every corner of his mind. He was suddenly certain that Zen wasn't entirely human.

"Are you okay, Gid?" Zen inquired, his words couched in concern. There was a noticeable furrow in his sun-bleached brows, his sea-glass green eyes reflecting an ocean of worry.

"Uh, it's… I'm just not sleeping well lately," Gideon lied, finding a plausible reason to placate the man in front of him.

Mustering up a small grin, Gideon kept his expression politely bland as he rang up the surfboard wax. As Zen stood closer now, leaning on the counter, Gideon could see the iridescent scales in greater detail. They bore an uncanny resemblance to ghostly tattoos, shifting and shimmering with every move Zen made, like a mirage dancing on his bronzed skin. His heart pounded in his chest, a frantic drumbeat that underscored his growing unease. "You really do love the ocean, don't you?" Gideon inquired, striving for a casual tone. "Surfing… you do it every day?"

Zen gave Gideon a nonchalant shrug and an easy grin. "If I can, yeah," he replied. "I try to get in the water every day."

"You're in it so much, you could practically be a merman," Gideon replied, chuckling at his joke but carefully watching as Zen jerked and gave him a startled, almost scared look. As quickly as the expression appeared on Zen's face, it slipped away.

Gideon finished the transaction and handed Zen a plastic bag. The man dipped his chin in thanks and quickly strode for the exit without another word. Gideon watched as he left. Right as Zen opened the door to leave, he turned back to Gideon with an almost worried look. Gideon quickly dropped his gaze before Zen caught him staring, pretending to be busy adjusting a display box of lip balms on the counter next to the register.

The rest of Gideon's shift at the gift shop was uneventful, the time stretching out interminably like an unending road, disappearing into the horizon under a relentless desert sun. His mind registered each tick of the clock with increasing monotony, the excitement of the morning's odd encounter a stark contrast to the mundane tedium that followed. The store was filled with the dull drone of shoppers' hushed conversations with the occasional chime of the cash register breaking the monotonous hum. His mind was elsewhere, filled with thoughts of Zen, Dacey, and the inexplicable ordeal they had found themselves in.

When the afternoon employees finally arrived, Gideon let out a breath he hadn't realized he'd been holding. He shot a text to Dacey, his fingers rapidly moving across the touchscreen. *Will be done in 30. Do you still need my help?*

In a matter of seconds, Dacey responded. *I'll pick u up. My turn*

2 drive. The remark brought a weak smile to his face. It was strange to find comfort in such small exchanges, but comfort he found, nonetheless.

Winding down his shift was excruciatingly slow. He stood by as Jared diligently counted out the cash drawer. With each passing second, Gideon tapped his foot against the floor, his gaze glued to the clock on the wall above Jared's head. When Jared finished, Gideon couldn't help but let out a sigh of relief. He clocked out hastily, the words of his goodbye to his colleagues swallowed by the urgency.

Bright, blinding sunlight greeted him as he stepped out of the shop, bathing the parking lot in a golden glow. He squinted, shielding his eyes and leaning against his car.

A grin spread across his face when Dacey's blue sedan pulled into the parking lot.

CHAPTER 18

Gideon hopped into the passenger seat, turning a vent to blow the air conditioning onto his overheated face. He turned to Dacey. "Hey, good afternoon. Anything exciting happen since I saw you yesterday?"

She shook her head, her nose scrunched up in annoyance like a disgruntled cat being offered off-brand kibble. "I tried to find any connection between Kaminski, Leroux, and Eglin golf course, but other than Leroux occasionally golfing there – nothing. And as far as I can determine, Kaminski and Leroux have nothing more than a passing knowledge of one another through their respective jobs. Their friend and family circles don't overlap. But I'm pretty certain that they are both up to their armpits in whatever is happening to these college students."

"So, what's the plan now?"

Dacey chewed on her thumbnail, her face thoughtful. "Let's head back to Niceville. I have a couple of the victims' home addresses. I want to look at their places and talk to their families and roommates if we can. See if any doctors or police officers had been hanging around before they turned up dead. I'm betting not, but it doesn't hurt to check. However, my real goal is to get you close enough to their places to see if you can pick up any traces of magic."

Nodding, Gideon relaxed back in the seat as Dacey pulled the car out of the parking lot and headed back toward town. Gideon shifted in his seat, turning his attention away from the scenery outside his window and looked at the Mythical woman driving next to him. He parted his lips, then pressed them together again before starting to speak. "Earlier today," he began, "I think I had an encounter with a merman."

Dacey's eyes showed surprise, then curiosity. Gideon continued, "There is this local guy named Zen I see occasionally. For the first time today, I noticed he had a strange aura and I swear I saw scales on his skin. Like fish scales. Do mermaids actually exist?"

Dacey gave Gideon a pleased grin, like she was proud of him for some reason. "Yes, merfolk totally exist. There's a lot of them in Florida because they need to be near the water, so there's a good chance this Zen guy is one. There are quite a few water-oriented Mythicals that he could possibly be – like a siren or a kraken shifter or maybe a selkie..."

Before Gideon could ask a thousand questions about kraken shifters, Dacey clucked her tongue. "Wait, you said scales, yeah?" When Gideon nodded, she continued, "Not a selkie then. There are other Mythicals with scales that aren't water-oriented too, like basilisks or dragons."

Once more, the world had broadened in a rather unexpected and fantastical way for Gideon. His gaze flicked to the road ahead as he digested this information. When Dacey noticed Gideon's stupefied expression, she laughed good-naturedly and promised to get him a Mythical 'guidebook' once they got through their current case.

Gideon watched Dacey as she drove, able to observe her without getting caught. He had initially written her off as abrasive – a pretty but tough-as-nails hardass. But as he watched her weave in and out of traffic, good-naturedly telling Gideon about some of the different Mythicals that he could expect to meet in a beach town, he saw a gentler side of her start to shine through. Her eyes shone with mirth, a warm glow that made the day brighter. A smile often found its way to her face, replacing her default scowl, softening her features, and making her look younger and more relaxed. Gideon smiled to himself; Dacey Menet was quite warm once one got past her blazing exterior.

With Dacey by his side, who alternated between being a tough mentor and a warm, supportive friend, Gideon began to accept the preternatural world unfolding around him.

It wasn't long before they were pulling up to a newer model house in an upper-middle-class neighborhood. It had a fancy brick facade and tons of large windows. It was one of those houses his mom liked to watch on the house-flipping television shows where they used words like 'open floor plan' and 'en-suite bathrooms'.

Dacey pulled the car into the driveway of the elegant residence, an older minivan parked out front at odds with the fancy house. Gideon got out of the car and followed her up the driveway. Curiosity got the better of him as he stopped next to the minivan and peered through the car's window, catching glimpses of scattered crumbs and colorful toys.

As she rang the doorbell, Gideon hung back slightly, observing their surroundings. There was a moment of silence and then Gideon heard a series of thumps before the door swung open. In the doorway was a pre-teen boy who stared at them with suspicious eyes.

Instantly, an otherworldly sensation washed over Gideon, stirring some deep instinct within him. The wave of magic engulfing his senses felt animalistic and primal in nature. He could almost feel coarse fur under his fingertips, an untamed wildness lingering in the air. When he gasped in reaction, the boy's suspicious stare deepened.

"Hey kid, is your mom home? Tell her someone from the Conclave is here to speak to her," Dacey quickly interjected, covering for Gideon's bizarre behavior.

"Mom!" the boy bellowed. "There's two people from the Conclave here to speak to you!"

With that overly loud announcement, the boy scampered off, leaving the door wide open. Gideon glanced around behind them, wondering if the neighbors heard the boy's yell.

Gideon heard an aggravated, feminine voice reprimand the boy a moment before a harried, plump woman appeared in the doorway. Again, Gideon felt that same wild magic.

"Can I help you?" the woman asked. She turned her attention toward Dacey, somehow instinctively knowing who was in charge. That gave Gideon a chance to really look at her. He immediately noticed the dark circles around her eyes and the air of grief clinging to her. She had the look of someone who was barely hanging on.

"Hi, Mrs. Sousa. My name is Candace Menet, and this is Gideon Bean. We've been sent by the Conclave to investigate the circumstances of your daughter's death."

Tears filled the woman's eyes but didn't spill over. "I told you people that my Aurelia would never touch drugs. Never. Something bad happened to her and the police won't listen to me."

"And that's why we're here. I know how hard this has all been for you and your family, but we are here to figure out what really happened. And I promise you that we won't quit until we uncover the truth. Whatever that may be."

Dacey's ability to turn on the charm astounded Gideon. She was so good at it that he wondered who the real Dacey was – the snarky hardass or the compassionate sincere woman in front of him.

Mrs. Sousa sniffed and ran a hand under her eyes to wipe away the tears. "Won't you please come in?" She stepped back and showed them into her living room, waving them to a couch.

Gideon and Dacey sat side by side on the plush loveseat, turning their focus on the frazzled woman across from them. Gideon's eyes darted from the woman's watery gaze to the remnants of a once tidy living room. The house, though showing signs of recent neglect, still possessed an air of former orderliness. As Gideon absentmindedly brushed aside some crumbs on the sofa, he couldn't help but notice the old pizza box and discarded clothing scattered on the floor, evidence of disarray.

Interrupting the pregnant silence, the woman's voice broke through, her words dripping with equal parts weariness and determination. "What can I do to help?"

Dacey leaned forward, her voice laced with concern. "I just need you to answer a few questions for us." When Mrs. Sousa bobbed her head to indicate that she was ready, Dacey began. "Had your daughter been spending time with anyone new recently? Acting secretive, perhaps? Anything out of the ordinary?"

The woman huffed, her frustration surfacing abruptly. Her eyes flashed with a mix of anger and exhaustion as she snapped back, "I've already answered these questions with the cops. They were nothing but jerks to me."

Dacey gave her a patient, empathetic look. "I understand that. And I understand how frustrated you must feel. But please answer my questions. You never know what small detail might be the thing that helps us solve this."

Mrs. Sousa took a deep breath, her face a mask of misery that made Gideon's gut clench.

"No, Aurelia wasn't hanging around anyone new. She wasn't dating anyone. There is no angry ex-boyfriend. She wasn't being secretive or disappearing or acting any different than normal. She goes to school full-time and has – had – a part-time job. Nothing was out of the ordinary. I've spent countless hours trying to find anything that was unusual and there's nothing. She went to a bar with a couple of her girlfriends to celebrate a good grade on a test. She got separated from her friends when they decided to go to a different bar. But she never showed up where they were supposed to meet, and they just assumed that she'd gone home. That's it. The cops tried to tell me that she must've gone off to do drugs. She was found in a bad part of town with a needle in her arm. They heavily implied that she must've done it with a man. The jerks behaved like she was a promiscuous party girl. But I know my daughter and she would have never done this – no matter how drunk she may have been. Never. She was scared of needles! And her friends said that she'd only had a beer or two."

"Do the names Alan Kaminski or Claude Leroux mean anything to you?"

Mrs. Sousa shook her head.

"Does your daughter golf?" Gideon piped up.

Mrs. Sousa reared back, giving Gideon an incredulous look. "No. Never."

Dacey nodded subtly at Gideon before she turned her attention back to the grieving mother. "Have you ever noticed any policemen or doctors hanging around your daughter?"

The woman wrinkled her nose at the turn of Dacey's questioning. She shook her head. "Not that I know of. Do you think the police were behind this? Is that why they didn't really investigate despite my pushing?"

"No, ma'am. I was just curious about the type of people that your daughter spent her time with."

Mrs. Sousa hunched over her knees, wringing her hands together in her lap as she spoke in a trembling voice. "Aurelia, she, uh… she didn't hang around with many people outside of our family and pack. We try to stick together." She sniffed, absently rubbing at her eyes. "There were a few friends from her class," she continued slowly, as if the effort to do so physically pained her. "Mostly just study partners. They helped each other practice for their exams. There were three of them: Mandy, Bethany, Jason. Smart kids. I've met them."

Gideon nodded, encouraging her to go on despite the visible pain etched on her face.

"And she had a couple of friends at work too, uh… Belinda and Roxanne," Mrs. Sousa added, her voice quavering. "They worked at the same cafe, you see. They would carpool together sometimes or cover shifts for each other. Just a friendly bunch, really. Those girls were my Aurelia's friends – always looking out for each other."

There was a heavy pause, Mrs. Sousa seeming to gather herself before she continued. "She was cautious, like me. Kept her circles small, didn't stray far from her safety net. I knew all these people, trusted them. They are… good kids."

Gideon felt bad as he watched the heartbreak in the woman's eyes.

Dacey cleared her throat. "Mrs. Sousa, Gideon here is an auramancer, and I am hoping he might be able to offer more assistance as we continue to look into your daughter's death."

"An auramancer?" Mrs. Sousa murmured. "I don't think I've ever met one of your kind before."

"Well, he's still in training but his magic is strong, and he was the only one who could get here right away," Dacey replied. Gideon didn't like that she was stretching the truth, but he knew that correcting her now would only muddy the waters of helping Mrs. Sousa and her daughter. He promised himself that he would say something to Dacey about lying when they were alone later. After the way lies had ruined his reputation once, he felt that honesty needed to be kept if he was going to continue working with Dacey.

Mrs. Sousa gave Gideon an intrigued look. "So, you can sense my magic?"

"I think so. I'm picking up something in this house."

"What are you picking up?" Mrs. Sousa asked, sitting forward, and staring at him. He was so glad to see a glimmer in her eyes through the sadness that he was happy to play along.

"Um, your magic feels... like, I get a sense of something primal and... animal-like?" He mentally crossed his fingers, hoping that description wasn't offensive. When Mrs. Sousa didn't object, Gideon closed his eyes and cocked his head, trying to get a better sense of Mrs. Sousa's aura. "I feel like I'm running through a forest, quiet and deadly, chasing down prey. I get a sense of thick fur... and sharp claws. Don't take this the wrong way, but your magic feels kinda predatory."

Gideon's eye popped open, chagrined at his too-honest words. Maybe Dacey's approach was better than his. He really hoped he hadn't just insulted this poor grieving woman. However, when his gaze met hers, she gave him a pleased smile as if he'd just complimented her.

"I'm a wolf shifter. So is my whole family, including Aurelia."

Gideon's eyes widened in delight. A werewolf. Mrs. Sousa was a real-life werewolf.

Gideon was about to ask about full moons when Dacey interjected, "Mrs. Sousa, would you mind if Gideon went to your daughter's room? We just want to see if he can sense any unusual magic that she might've encountered."

Mrs. Sousa stood up. "Of course. Follow me."

Gideon and Dacey exchanged knowing glances, before following Mrs. Sousa down a hallway leading off the living room.

Mrs. Sousa and Dacey stayed back once Gideon was shown Aurelia's bedroom. The space could have been any college-age woman's room: A basket of laundry waiting on a chair. A small desk with a computer and a haphazard stack of books. A vanity mirror lined with pictures of smiling people. A pretty girl with a happy smile and long, dark hair was in most of the photos.

Closing his eyes again, Gideon stood in the middle of the room and rolled out his senses. All he felt was the same magic as

Mrs. Sousa's – magic that screamed wolf, now that he knew what he was sensing.

As he worked, he couldn't help but overhear Dacey quietly assuring a sniffling Mrs. Sousa. "We're going to do everything we can to figure out what happened to Aurelia."

"You promise?" was her watery response.

"Yes, I promise. We might not solve her murder, but I promise that we will do everything in our power to figure it out."

Gideon swallowed thickly and silently added his own vow to Dacey's. He would see this through and find both Aurelia – and Dacey's – killer. No matter what.

Wanting to be thorough, Gideon slowly walked the perimeter of the room, stopping often to push his senses out. Opening his eyes, his gaze clashed with Dacey's expectant one. He shook his head, disappointed to let her down.

He turned to the woman hovering anxiously in the doorway, watching his every move. "Mrs. Sousa, do you have anything that had been on your daughter the night she died?"

The woman nodded. "Yes, they gave me back her purse, although both her wallet and phone are missing. Would that work?"

Gideon flashed Dacey a quick, triumphant grin. "Yes, that would be perfect."

"Is it in here?" Gideon asked, looking back at the bedroom.

Mrs. Sousa shook her head. "It's in my bedroom. Here, follow me."

As Mrs. Sousa led Gideon and Dacey to the master bedroom, anticipation filled Gideon's gut. With a gentle push, the door swung open, revealing a spacious room with more photos on the wall. The same woman was featured in many of the large prints, surrounded by her family. Gideon's eyes immediately pulled toward a wide chest of drawers. Without prompting from Mrs. Sousa, he carefully maneuvered towards it.

On top of the dresser was more piled clothing. Something

dark and insidious tugged at him from underneath. Carefully, he brushed aside some clothes revealing a small pink backpack-like purse. Time seemed to momentarily stand still as he stared at the purse that reeked of familiar magic. Seeking confirmation, Gideon looked at Mrs. Sousa and asked, "It's hers, isn't it?"

Mrs. Sousa nodded, her face betraying a hint of anxiety mixed with hope.

Intrigued by the pulsating magic that seemed to emanate from the purse, Gideon hesitated. Turning to Dacey, a silent understanding passed between them. She raised her eyebrows. Gideon met her gaze, dipping his chin once.

Mrs. Sousa's face transformed from apprehension to desperate hope. Taking a step closer, she clasped onto Dacey's arm, seeking reassurance. Her voice trembled as she pleaded, "You found something? Please, tell me."

Dacey's voice quivered with tempered excitement as she explained their discovery. "It's a potential lead. There is no guarantee that this will lead to anything, so I don't want to give you false hope." Too late, Gideon thought with a smidge of chagrin. "It might turn out to be nothing. But... we're going to keep looking into this, okay? You understand that I can't make you any promises except that we will try."

Mrs. Sousa nodded, her expression desperate. He dreaded the thought of letting her down.

With a few promises to Mrs. Sousa that they would let her know the results of their investigation, Gideon and Dacey headed out of the house and got into the car.

Before Dacey could start the vehicle, Gideon turned to her, ire filling his voice. "You told Mrs. Sousa that I was being trained and that I was the nearest auramancer which is why I was there. That was a lie. You lied about needing a ride yesterday. You lied to Mrs. Sousa. I can't work with you if you keep lying, especially to me, Dacey. I won't. No matter what the reason, you're on your own if you keep lying. I mean it," he asserted, his voice firm and resolute. "I won't stand for it again. Just be honest with me from now on or I'm out."

She nodded, her expression solemn. "Alright, I understand. Seriously. I hear you, Gideon. It won't happen again. I pinkie swear."

A playful smirk tugged at Dacey's lips as she held up her hand, pinkie extended, the tilt of her eyebrows suggesting it was more of a tease than a serious offer. Yet, Gideon, hooked her slender, warm pinkie with his. His gray eyes met hers with a solid, unyielding intensity. "I am holding you to your word, Dacey," he told her, his voice resounding inside the car.

"Deal," Dacey said. "You have my word. Now let's head to the next victim's house."

Gideon and Dacey spent the rest of the afternoon driving around the panhandle, visiting the homes of the victims. It had been a painful, somber tour through a line-up of bereaved households, each one heavy with the weight of unspeakable loss.

At each residence, Dacey introduced herself as a private investigator hired to determine if foul play might have been a factor in their family member's death or disappearance. Her revelation was met with a tide of gratitude and desperation, an eager flood of cooperation from grieving families. The authorities' investigation, it seemed, had left much to be desired. Their seething disappointment was palpable.

About half of the dead or missing were human college students. The others were Mythicals, most of them were shifters. When Gideon asked about it, Dacey explained that shifters were the most common type of Mythical. One of the victims had been a hedgewitch named Susan, whose family clutched at Dacey's promise of a renewed inquiry like a lifeline. Gideon had walked out of the house with the scent of herbs in his nose and the feeling of green growing plants under his skin.

At Dacey's prompting, Gideon had walked around each house – some old suburban homes, some modern, blocky apartments, and a few modest townhomes. His hands had flicked over each item that once belonged to the deceased as his inner senses searched voraciously for the residue of the malevolent energy.

He noticed the way his skin tingled whenever he neared an object with traces of magic, like static electricity playing over his flesh. Yet nothing felt like the malignant rot he was searching for.

It was late afternoon as Gideon and Dacey approached the final house. It was an ancient antebellum manor, grand columns flanking the wide inviting porch. Hesitant, he watched as Dacey rang the doorbell.

An actual butler answered the door, leaving Gideon staring in shock. Once Dacey explained their purpose for stopping by, the reserved look dropped off the man's face. The butler was a rail-thin man, skin stretched tautly over his bony frame, with his white hair formed into a perfect sweep across his forehead.

"Please wait here while I fetch Mr. and Mrs. Whetan," the man said before striding quickly away.

Gideon stood in the open double doors of the sprawling mansion, taking a deep breath as he readied himself. He pushed his senses into the house, practicing like Dacey had instructed him to. He extended his auramancer powers into the wooden structure, feeling the energy in the building fill his senses, like water poured from a pitcher. It was unlike any sensation he'd encountered yet – powerful, fluid, and strangely alluring. It hummed with an energy that drew him in closer, seemingly pulling at the marrow in his bones, demanding compliance.

Dacey watched him closely. "What are you sensing?" she asked, her voice barely above a whisper. He could hear the curiosity knitted in her inquiry, laced with a hint of caution.

"It's… hard to explain," Gideon replied, his brows furrowing in concentration. The sensation was like the push and pull of a tidal current, demanding that he give in and be swept away. "It's powerful. It has an energy that pulls at me, coercing me... almost as if it's trying to bend me to its will."

Dacey nodded, a faint approving smile twitching at her lips, the sight itself as enigmatic as the power they were discussing. Gideon raised an eyebrow at her.

"This place belongs to a Fae family," Dacey clarified, her voice firm. "They're known for manipulating emotions. It's sort of their... specialty."

Gideon blinked in surprise, mulling over her revelations. The strange tantalizing sensation made more sense now, sending a chill down his spine as he contemplated the implications. He'd suspected Dacey would shatter his reality, but so far, it was exceeding even his most outlandish expectations.

The unmistakable pounding of heavy footsteps rang down a dimly lit hallway, and a set of oak double doors swung open. Gideon and Dacey swiveled around simultaneously, met with the sight of the old butler. Two unfamiliar figures trailed in his wake: an elegant yet somber couple who appeared to be in their mid-sixties.

The woman, adorned in a pastel peach pantsuit, approached first. Her cobalt blue eyes met Gideon's hesitantly as she adjusted the clutch of her hand around her partner's sleeve, holding on as if it were the only thing anchoring her to earth. "Are you here... about Tabitha?" her voice trembled from uncertainty.

Dacey, standing tall beside Gideon, calmly affirmed, "Yes, we are."

A wave of palpable relief washed over the couple and, for a second, the woman's grip on the man's arm seemed to loosen a touch. The premature lines of worry embedded into their features seemed less prominent, and their shoulders sagged, as though relieved of a massive burden.

As Dacey went through her now-familiar set of questions, Gideon found himself losing interest. It wasn't the repetition making him zone out, but instead, it was the unusual energy emanating from the couple. It felt chaotic, a swirling vortex of raw and untamed power, like wind carrying the scent of an impending storm. The strength of it hummed against his senses, an unseen force making the hairs on the back of his neck stand on end.

Gideon had been mulling over the sensation, mentally filing it under 'Fae manipulator' in his mind, when the sudden swell of energy prickled along his spine. His attention was abruptly yanked back into the present where the tides of magic began to coalesce around Dacey and the imposing figure of Tabitha's father. The man was a tempest, his aura like a swirling maelstrom filling the charged environment.

"Whatever it takes, Miss Menet," he commanded, his voice catching on the grit of desperation. "Find who murdered my girl and bring them to justice. No matter the cost."

His words cracked like a whip, sending unseen ripples through the tense air of the office. A feral snarl twisted Gideon's lips, instinctive protectiveness flaring in his chest. In three strides, he was blocking the man's path to Dacey.

"Stop that!" Gideon interjected sharply.

The torrent of magic swirling around them paused at Gideon's fierce outburst, the energy around them stuttering in surprise. But before he could respond, Dacey stepped up next to Gideon, giving Mr. Whetan a deadly glare.

Gideon stood his ground, his shoulders squared and his eyes blazing with defensive anger. With a grudging nod of acknowledgment, Mr. Whetan backed down.

"He's an auramancer," Dacey explained softly, her gaze steady on the agitated, bereaved father. "He can sense the shifts in your magic, the pressure of your commands. If I informed the Conclave that you tried to use your influence on one of their agents…"

Mr. Whetan looked like he'd swallowed a brick. His wife stepped forward, her hand outstretched beseechingly to Dacey.

"We're sorry. He didn't mean it. We're just so desperate to find out what really happened to Tabitha."

Dacey huffed out a sigh. "I understand, Mrs. Whetan – believe me, I really do. However, if you try a stunt like that again, I will be forced to report you. Do you understand?"

The parents nodded like frantic bobblehead dolls.

"I have a final question before Mr. Bean here checks your residence… Do you have anything personal that Tabitha had on her the night she died?"

"Yes," Mrs. Whetan murmured, her face pale even in the dimness of the unlit foyer. "We were able to retrieve a necklace that Tabitha had been wearing… on the night."

Before she could further explain, she turned on her heels and dashed off, disappearing temporarily into the doors they'd arrived through. Gideon waited, a coil of dread and confusion wound tight within him. He didn't have long to wait, however. Mrs. Whetan returned holding a small velvet box. She handed it to him with trembling fingers, delicately avoiding any direct eye contact.

Opening the box, the sight that met his eyes sent a shiver down his spine. Nestled within the protective confines of the box was a necklace. Its thin delicate chain was gold, polished bright. Plucking the necklace from the velvet it was cradled upon, Gideon held it in his cupped hands, the weight of it heavier than he expected.

He finally felt it – a familiar sickening sensation, like poison creeping its way under his skin. Gideon recoiled, pausing to brace himself against a ragged breath.

The twisted magic at his fingertips confirmed his suspicions; he looked up from the necklace and gave Dacey a knowing look, even as the magic in his palm twisted his stomach.

Once they finished checking over the residence, they left with a final promise to the Whetans to do as much as possible to find out the true circumstances of their daughter's death. As soon as they got back in the car, Dacey made a call, her eyes flashing with intensity. "Wiz, when will the team be getting here?"

Gideon couldn't help but overhear the conversation, his curiosity piqued. He strained his ears as Dacey started the engine.

Wiz's voice crackled over the minuscule speaker, her tone professional. "They should be there later tonight, Dacey. So did you find something?"

Dacey told Wiz about what they had discovered so far. "Because of Gideon, we can conclusively link the magic from Kaminski and Leroux's houses to objects that were on two of the victims when they died. I think that's enough to have both men brought in for questioning."

Gideon hid a wince at The Wiz's next words. "Are you sure you can trust his senses? He hasn't been tested. It could be a fluke."

Dacey cut her eyes over to Gideon's, meeting his stare with a steady gaze. "Yeah, Wiz, I trust his magic."

Gideon couldn't hear the rest of what Dacey was saying over the buzzing in his ears. He couldn't imagine how stupid the expression was on his face, but he couldn't help it. Before Dacey, the only person who truly believed in him was his mom. And mothers were contractually obligated to believe in their children, even if they didn't deserve it, so it hardly counted.

Once the call ended, Gideon could feel Dacey's gaze on him before she even spoke. "I can take you home, Gideon," she offered. "You should get some rest before your shift at the crematorium tonight."

"You sure you don't need any more help?" Gideon asked, trying to keep the hopeful tone out of his voice.

Dacey shook her head, a gentle but firm refusal. "We probably won't need any more help from you," she replied. "But if we do, rest assured, I'll contact you."

Gideon nodded in understanding, even though the thought of being left out of the ongoing action stung. But he hid it well, giving her a small smile as he accepted her proposal. "Alright then," he conceded before turning away to stare at the passing scenery outside the car window. He was almost surprised to see how close to his home they already were. He knew his job was done, but a part of him wasn't ready to step back just yet. His life had seen more excitement in these past few days than it had in years. Now, all he could do was wait and see what the new day would bring.

CHAPTER 20

*L*ater that night, Gideon stood in the dimly lit cremation room, music blasting in his ears with sweat pouring down his back. The air conditioning was on the fritz again, and coupled with heat from retort ovens, it was sweltering. He had to stop often just to stand inside the walk-in fridge with the corpses to cool off.

He'd performed his duties at the crematorium countless times before, the repetitive nature of the job allowing his mind to wander. Normally he just daydreamed, but today, Dacey and the perplexing case they'd been working on consumed his thoughts. When he'd gotten home that afternoon, he'd checked his email and found a message from Leonhard Gauss at Nexus Consulting Services, including a document with information about aura-mancers waiting for him. He'd opened the attached file and tried to read it, but the arcane and instruction manual-style document on the powers of an auramancer soon had his eyes crossing. He'd quickly decided that he needed a full night's sleep before he could start to decipher the document that was supposed to explain how his magic worked.

Lost in his own musings, Gideon's eyes scanned over the next cremation permit absentmindedly until a familiar name suddenly jolted him out of his reverie: Leroux. It struck him like a lightning bolt.

With only a moment's hesitation, Gideon turned and grabbed the associated death certificate from a nearby table. He studied the document intently, his eyes widening as he confirmed his suspicions. The coroner who had signed both the permit and the death certificate was none other than Leroux. Next, he snatched up the cremation authorization form, and his gut instinct was confirmed when he saw that Kaminski had given the stamp of approval.

With the paperwork clutched tightly in his hand, Gideon walked over to the refrigerator and scanned the corpse-filled boxes inside. He instinctively was drawn to a box in the back corner of the fridge. Now that he was paying attention, a miasma of foul magic clung to the box that he was annoyed that he hadn't noticed sooner. He couldn't believe that he forgot to pay attention to his senses. His magic was a muscle he wasn't used to flexing.

Lifting the lid, he reared back, gagging as the feeling of queasy darkness bloomed out of the opening. Once he got himself back under control, he looked inside the box and found a body wrapped in white cloth. With a weird swoopy feeling cramping his stomach, he went back to his workstation and snatched up a pair of scissors from a drawer. The death certificate stated that the body within that box belonged to the man whose death had been ruled an accident because of a fatal fall in his own home.

He had a moment's apprehension about what he was about to do. Deviating from the cremation process could lose him this job if anyone ever found out.

"Shit," he groaned. "I have to check."

Berating himself for his hesitation, Gideon stepped up to the box and began cutting through the cloth, starting at the corpse's feet. A middle-aged man was finally revealed. The gaping wound across the man's thick neck made Gideon loudly cuss.

Gideon was dialing Dacey's number before the fridge door finished swinging closed behind him.

The phone rang three times before Dacey's groggy voice came over the line. "You better have a damn good reason for waking me at two in the morning, Giddy."

Gideon ignored the nickname, too worried about the body in the fridge to chastise her. "I have a body here in the crematorium fridge whose throat has been cut. You'll never guess who filled out the death certificate stating that the man died from an accidental fall."

The fuzziness from Dacey's voice disappeared. "Holy shit. Give me thirty minutes, and I'll be right there."

When a loud knock sounded from the front door, it had only been twenty minutes. Dacey must've driven like a bat out of hell to make it from her hotel to the crematorium in that amount of time.

Stepping into the front office, he quickly unlocked the door and ushered her inside. "Where's your car? Did you park out back?"

Dacey nodded, following Gideon to the fridge.

"I checked over the rest of our docket for tonight, and Leroux signed off on three other death certificates aside from this one," Gideon explained, handing the first certificate to Dacey. "Of the others, there was one other that didn't match the cause of death – at least as far as I could tell. And both stunk to high heaven of dark magic."

Dacey took one look at the two bodies that Gideon had discovered, both with gaping raw wounds across their throats, and growled in a way that made him want to take a step back. She stared at the bodies for a moment before turning back to Gideon. "I called the team on my way, and they should be here shortly. I need to call them back and give them an update."

Stalking out of the fridge, Dacey was already making the call. "Hey, yeah, I just looked at the bodies and Gideon's right, we've got a situation. We know who two of the perpetrators are. Yeah, that's right, Kaminski and Leroux. Yeah, they're the ones I warned you about earlier. I want them in custody before breakfast – send the retrieval teams to apprehend them both before anyone else gets killed. I don't care. We need to find out if they're working with anyone else." Dacey paused and looked back at Gideon. "Druids? I mean, maybe… but I don't think so. It doesn't look like their work – I haven't seen a single rune. Oh yeah, I heard about that mess in Cascadia. Can you reach out to the local Grove and see if they know these guys? Unless they're unregistered, they'd be on the roster. Also, I need a forensic team sent to Peterson Cremation Services in Gulf Breeze immediately. How fast can you get them here?" Dacey paused for a moment, making eye contact with Gideon. "Hey, Gideon, what time does the owner normally come in?"

"Um, typically, Mr. Peterson is here by 8. He and Linus are both scheduled to work tomorrow morning."

"Did you hear that? I need the team here before 8, much sooner if possible. Can we make that happen? Perfect, even sooner than I'd hoped. Oh! Quinn is with you, right? Perfect, we're gonna need a truth seeker. I want the owner of this place questioned. Send me an ETA when you can."

Once Dacey hung up the call, she turned to Gideon. "Do you guys store copies of the cremation records?"

"Um, yeah, I think so. I think we keep the records here for a couple of years. After that, I don't know if they get stored somewhere else or destroyed."

"We have at least an hour before the team arrives. I'd like to look through those a bit before they get here."

Gideon led Dacey to the small storage room that contained the records. A single dim light from the hall cast long shadows on the rows of metal cabinets. Flipping on an overhead light as they entered the space, Gideon pointed to the drawer with the most recent cremation records. Dacey rubbed her hands together, her eyes lit up with anticipation.

"Let's see what we can find," Dacey murmured as she started thumbing quickly through the files, her fingers moving swiftly.

Gideon cleared his throat. "You said something about druids on your call..."

Dacey looked up from the manila folder she'd been examining. "A few of months ago, a couple of druid brothers in the northwest region of the country got caught sacrificing people."

"Why would they do that? What do they gain from it?"

"Usually power. There's powerful magic to be gained from blood sacrifices."

"And you think that's what's happening here?"

Dacey nodded. "It's what I suspect, anyway. Cutting someone's throat is the quick way to get their blood."

"What's a... a Grove?" Gideon asked, hoping he remembered the word correctly.

"That is what a group of druids are called."

Suddenly, Dacey halted. Slowly, she removed a file, staring at it intently for a moment before looking up and meeting Gideon's gaze.

She held the folder out for him to see, her eyes blazing with triumph. "I know this name. Alexander Bauer. He was one of the university students whose death was flagged suspicious by Leonhard."

"That's the guy who sent me an email with information about being an auramancer. What did you say he was again?"

"Leonhard's a Numerai," Dacey responded, her tone absentminded as she continued to paw through the filing cabinet. She flipped open another folder and started scanning through the contents, her brows furrowed.

With a low curse, Dacey looked up at Gideon. Turning the folder, she pointed to a signature at the bottom of a form. "Look who signed the death certificate," she said with a touch of sarcasm. "Surprise, surprise, it's Leroux." Glancing back inside the folder, she flipped to the next form. She chuckled, shaking her head. "And you're never going to guess who signed the cremation authorization form. If you said Kaminski, you'd win a cookie." Setting the folder on a nearby surface, Dacey turned back to the cabinet. "Let's see if we can find the rest."

Thirty minutes later, Dacey had located the files for all seven university students that she had been investigating. Every single one had been autopsied by Dr. Claude Leroux and the cremation authorization forms had been signed off by Officer Alan Kaminski.

Dacey stared at the stack of folders for a long minute, biting her lip. She turned to Gideon with a sigh. "It's not proof, but it's super suspicious. Certainly enough to justify pulling in the team. Let's go through all the files you have and pull out any folders where Leroux and Kaminski both signed off on them. We'll make a separate pile of those potential victims while we wait for everyone."

By the time a loud knock on the front door jolted them out of their search, they had a stack of fourteen additional files set aside. Dacey shook her head like she was trying to wake up from a trance. Glancing at her watch, she gave Gideon a wide grin. "Right on time. Come on, Giddy, let me introduce you to the team."

"Gideon," he corrected, instinctively knowing that it was a useless endeavor.

Dacey quickly strode out of the records room. Gideon dropped the folder he'd been looking at back into the filing cabinet and rushed to follow.

He caught up to Dacey just as she entered the front lobby. His eyes caught on the four people waiting outside the front door, partially hidden in the shadowy darkness of the late hour. Standing just outside the glass front doors were two women and two men. Before he could get much of a look at them, Dacey was unlocking the door and waving them inside.

Dacey's fiery eyes lit up, her excitement evident. "Hey, guys! I'm so glad you could make it." Her genuine warmth enveloped the air as she exchanged enthusiastic greetings with the newcomers. Gideon stood back, feeling awkward, especially since Dacey seemed so nice and relaxed around them. He was chagrined to realize that he was a jealous moron who wanted the same warmth from Dacey that these strangers were receiving. Gideon imagined punching himself in the face for being such a clingy idiot. It was a very bad idea to get attached to the mercurial bennu shifter who was, at best, a temporary work partner who barely tolerated his presence because she wanted to use his powers.

A curly-haired woman, who reminded Gideon of a middle-aged soccer mom with her messy hair bun and huge travel coffee mug, hugged Dacey tightly. "You know I wouldn't miss this for the world, Dace!" she exclaimed, her familiar voice filled with energy despite the late hour.

Dacey then turned to the other woman, who had dark hair cut into a bob, her tone shifting to a more serious note. "We have some important information to share. It's about the recent deaths and what we've uncovered." The black-haired woman nodded, her expression focused and determined. Her calm, reserved demeanor was an interesting contrast to the other woman's vivacious energy.

Gideon turned his attention away from the women and observed the two men. One was a thin, almost petite bespectacled man who, at first glance, seemed annoyed to be there, standing slightly away from the rest of the group. Gideon wondered if he was introverted too. The second man was a burly fellow who exuded an air of protective strength, steady and formidable.

Gideon immediately identified with the slight, nerdy-looking guy. The other man, with his bulk and demeanor, immediately made Gideon remember the jocks he'd carefully avoided back in high school.

Dacey gestured for everyone to follow her as she led the way to the records room. "Let's grab a table and discuss everything. We've got some work ahead of us," she declared, a mixture of determination and anticipation in her voice.

"Why don't you introduce us to your friend?" the curly-haired woman said to Dacey, bumping her with her elbow.

"Oh shit! Sorry, I'm just so focused on this case I forgot."

The curly-haired woman slipped past Dacey with her hand held out to Gideon. He gripped the offered hand. Her magic felt effervescent – like champagne bubbles popping against the palm of his hand.

"That's the Wiz – you talked to her on the phone earlier. She's the logistics and cleanup. She'll erase any trace of our presence once we're done here," Dacey said.

While Gideon shook Wiz's hand, Dacey pointed out the rest of the team. She indicated the woman with the short bob. "This is Quinn – she's our truth seeker."

"Truth seeker," Gideon repeated slowly, letting go of Wiz's hand.

Quinn didn't offer her hand to Gideon but gave him a quick, fleeting smile. "I can sense when someone lies. I can also get people to tell me the truth or unveil their secrets. I'm here to question the owner of this facility to see if he was a party to the crimes you're investigating. I'll also be questioning Kaminski and Leroux once they're apprehended. I've been told that my power feels like hypnosis. I will be interested to hear an auramancer's take."

Dacey pointed to the thin, bespectacled man. "That's MacGuire."

Gideon felt chagrined, he had assumed the slight, nerdy-looking man was Leonhard, the Numerai. He realized that he had no idea what Leonhard looked like and shouldn't have made assumptions. Leonhard might be a suave Casanova or a jock for all Gideon knew. He shouldn't assume that a Mythical with special math powers would look like a stereotypical geek.

"Don't ruin my fun, Dacey," MacGuire said with a slightly pompous smirk, transforming his face from reserved to smarmy in a single heartbeat. "I want him to guess what I am."

The name MacGuire was familiar, but it took Gideon a moment to place it – Dacey had said that she didn't want a man named MacGuire as her new handler; she'd said that she found him annoying.

Dacey rolled her eyes when Gideon glanced at her. Shrugging, Gideon held out his hand. He realized that he probably needed to prove himself to Dacey's team.

He felt a surprising firmness and an underlying grit to the man's magic, as if Gideon's palm had just grazed a weathered boulder. It reminded him of the feeling of running his hand across a brick wall. A sly smile played on MacGuire's lips as he looked at Gideon.

"Well? What am I?" He cocked an eyebrow as if expecting Gideon to fail his challenge.

Gideon took a moment to study MacGuire's narrow features, his sharp blue-eyed gaze, his pale complexion, and the shape of his mouth that held a certain smug disdain to it. Nothing about the man's face was giving Gideon the impression that matched the feeling of stone and rock that the slender man's handshake had conveyed.

Gideon hesitantly replied, "Rock troll?"

MacGuire raised an eyebrow, clearly amused by his guess. But Gideon also detected a hint of surprise.

"Not bad, not bad. I'm a gargoyle." He said that in a way that made Gideon believe that MacGuire thought the announcement should be very impressive.

"Gargoyle? Like the statues on a cathedral?"

Dacey sputtered out a laugh. MacGuire gave him a sour look. "No, the statues on churches are just carvings made of stone. The artists based those statues on actual gargoyles because we're a symbol of protection."

Gideon couldn't help but feel a smidge of respect as he looked at MacGuire. The thin, unassuming exterior held a hidden creature that was famous for its fierceness and strength.

It was too bad that MacGuire seemed like a smug jerk. It would've been cool to be friends with an actual gargoyle, but Gideon immediately sensed that he and MacGuire would probably never be friends.

"He's just the muscle, Gideon," Dacey said snidely, nudging him to turn away from MacGuire. Gideon could hear MacGuire's huff of annoyance at Dacey's words.

"And this is Santos," Dacey said, her voice switching back to a warm tone, tilting her head to indicate the beefy man standing at the back of the gathering. "He's an investigator with the FBI."

"I smooth over any cross-agency territorial disputes. I just flash my badge and the local cops get out of our way."

Dacey bumped her shoulder into Santos's side. "Pssh, you're more than that. He's a top-notch investigator. And almost as good with a computer as Leonhard."

"Uh, it's nice to meet you," Gideon said, holding out his hand and ignoring the kernel of jealousy in his idiotic gut at their obvious friendship.

With a small smile, Santos put his meaty hand in Gideon's. Gideon blinked several times when he immediately got the impression of vibration. It was like putting his hand on a washing machine and realizing it was on a spin cycle, feeling the invisible, frenetic motion.

"What'd you pick up, Gideon? I can tell you felt something," Santos asked, his smile kind and anticipatory.

"Uh, like, motion? Vibration and energy? It's hard to explain."

Santos gave him a wide grin. "Nah, that's great. You've got real talent. I'm a Fae. My ability is telekinesis. I can move things with just a thought."

Wiz elbowed her way past Santos, her eyes alight with excitement. "Wait, what did my magic feel like?"

Gideon tried his best to explain the feeling of her magic against his hand. He wasn't sure he could find the words to describe it, but he did his best.

"Ooh, champagne bubbles – I like that," Wiz crowed.

Dacey gave her a droll look. "Okay, Bubbles. We've got work to do. Enough of this game. Let me show you guys the bodies and then the paperwork we pulled."

"Can you get me access to the computers here, Gideon?" Santos asked.

As Gideon led the group back to the records room, Gideon couldn't help but feel a small surge of envy at the group's easy camaraderie.

CHAPTER 21

Gideon had spent countless nights in the crematorium, the hum of the ovens a constant companion, but he had never imagined that he would be scouring the very same place for evidence of sinister deeds. He watched Dacey, her fiery aura flickering softly around her in the dimly lit building.

He and Dacey's crew tossed the entire crematorium. He felt immense guilt because, from the investigation, it appeared that the crematorium had been burning bodies for Kaminski and Leroux for at least a couple of months. He felt like an accomplice, given that he'd unknowingly been erasing the evidence of murders.

Gideon pored over the records stashed away in the cramped filing cabinets until his eyes started to cross. Receipts, transaction records, and inventory spreadsheets, each offering an insight into the damning possibility that the owner had indeed been in cahoots with Leroux and Kaminski.

With each potential clue that they uncovered, he felt a strange mixture of dread and defiant determination stir within him. The crematorium, once a haven of solitude to him, now felt hauntingly ominous, a dark past lurking beneath the familiar sounds of the ovens and exhaust fans. There was one thing he knew for certain: nothing about his life would ever be the same again.

Needing a break from the cramped records room, Gideon found himself in Mr. Peterson's office standing behind Santos, silently watching him navigate through the accounting software. Gideon had never given any thought to what an FBI investigator actually did for their job – if pressed, he would've guessed car chases and armed standoffs – but he never imagined it had anything to do with scanning slowly through financial records. Time seemed to stretch as Santos meticulously scrutinized each journal entry, looking for a breakthrough that would expose Mr. Peterson as an accomplice.

When Santos had first sat at the desk, he'd dialed up Leonhard to help him gain access to Mr. Peterson's bank accounts. When Gideon mentioned that he was surprised that the Numerai hadn't arrived with the rest of the team, Santos laughed and said that Leonhard never left his "command center".

"I've never even met Leonhard face-to-face despite working with him for over ten years," Santos confided to Gideon.

Gideon had given Santos such an incredulous look that it had caused him to laugh loudly.

"Welcome to the Conclave, kid. We're all weird here."

Gideon hoped that he could form a friendship with the easy-going Fae man. He was still smiling to himself over Santos's effortless acceptance of him when Leonhard's voice came over the phone speaker and pulled Gideon's thoughts back into the present. "I'm in. I can't believe that this guy uses the same password for everything. Amateur hour, I swear." Gideon could hear the rapid click of a keyboard over the line. "Let's see if this guy has any unusual transactions in his personal bank account since the business transactions all seem to be on the up and up. I want to know if he's dirty before he comes to work. How long have I got, Gideon?"

Gideon looked at his watch, then out the window, surprised

at the time. The sky outside the windows of the crematorium's front office had started to lighten, signaling the start of a new day. "Uh, he should be in within the next thirty minutes."

Although Gideon didn't care much for Mr. Peterson, he had a hard time imagining the man taking money to help cover up murders.

Wiz came skipping into the room, looking pleased. "Hey, just got the news that Leroux has been taken into custody. Now that they have him secure, they're closing in on Kaminski next."

Santos looked up from the computer monitor and speared Wiz with a raised eyebrow. "What's taking so long? They should've had them in custody hours ago."

Wiz shrugged. "It took headquarters a while to assemble the right team. They were worried since we don't know what kind of Mythicals we're dealing with."

A few hours earlier, Gideon had found himself on a phone call with a woman named Vena, a fellow auramancer from South Carolina. Eager to understand the magic he experienced with Kaminski and Leroux, Gideon attempted to convey the sensation of the men's auras to her, hoping that he'd found someone who would understand what he'd experienced. Together, they speculated that Kaminski and Leroux might be druids or shadow mages, though she'd acknowledged that it was nothing more than a conjecture. She told Gideon to have Dacey bag up an item contaminated by the dark aura and have it sent to her, and she'd examine it to see if she could recognize the magic. The conversation left Gideon feeling relieved, as Vena seemed like a normal person and was kind to him. She had reassured Gideon that he could reach out anytime if he had further inquiries.

"Hey." Gideon managed to keep from jerking away when a voice came from beside him. He hadn't even noticed Wiz sidling up next to him.

Before he could even respond, Wiz started talking excitedly. "I've never been in a crematorium before, and I have so. Many.

Questions! Okay, first question – are the bodies always burned in cardboard boxes? For some reason, I kinda thought they'd be in caskets or something."

"Sometimes, but not usually. Since it will all be burnt into ash, most people don't waste money on a casket. Some people do get one, but that's usually because they have a viewing right before the cremation." Gideon pointed in the direction of the formal viewing room. "Since I work a graveyard shift, I don't get those clients. The viewings only happen during the day."

"Oh, that makes sense. Okay, next question: you ever get someone really obese?"

"Of course," Gideon responded. "We get a lot of overweight people because they can't fit into a standard casket. And getting a custom casket made is *very* expensive."

"You ever had anyone too big to fit in the oven?"

Gideon grinned in the face of Wiz's enthusiasm. "Not that I've ever heard of. Did you get a look at the retort ovens? They're damn big. If a person is overweight, we can cremate them, but it might cost the family more, because, obviously, it takes a lot longer to burn them down."

"How much do the ashes weigh once you're done?"

"Between four to eight pounds."

"That's crazy. So, like, the heavier the ashes are, the heavier the person was?"

"You'd think so, but no. Height is more of a determinant than being overweight when it comes to what the ashes weigh. Most of the fat gets completely burned off. Bone density factors in a lot more. The ashes are mostly made from the person's bones."

Leonhard's voice interrupted Wiz's next question. "Got it!" he crowed over the phone.

"Oh yeah? Whatcha got?" Santos asked, rolling his shoulders, and cracking his neck as if staring at a computer had given him a crick.

Leonhard's voice crackled with excitement as he relayed the

breakthrough. "It's all right here. Your boss has been receiving recurring monthly deposits to his personal bank account. What a moron. He's not even trying to cover his tracks," Leonhard scoffed. "How could he be so careless, leaving such a blatant trail behind? I will never understand these criminals. How can they be so arrogant to believe that they'll never get caught? The IRS would have caught this eventually, even without our help."

Gideon's attention snapped out the front window when he noticed Linus's truck pulling into the parking lot. "Shit! Linus is early."

"Linus? That's your co-worker?" Wiz asked.

"Yes. Linus Hartley – he works the day shift."

"Do you think he might be in on this?" Leonhard asked.

Gideon hesitated but ultimately shook his head. "I don't think so. He's loud and annoying, but I don't think he'd ever agree to hide murders. Although, to be honest, if you'd asked me that same question about Mr. Peterson, I would have said the same thing."

Santos stood up from the desk. "We'll find out either way. Everyone, head to the back, and when he comes in, I'll take him under custody. MacGuire, I want you as backup in case he gives us any trouble."

Gideon followed everyone as they shuffled out of the front office. He watched as Santos and MacGuire waited by the closed door that led from the front half of the crematorium to the restricted back half of the building. Gideon steeled himself mentally for the confrontation that was coming.

Gideon felt a flash of apprehension and guilt as he watched Santos pull a gun from a holster. He could already imagine how scary this was about to be for Linus. Everyone held their breath at the sound of the front door opening and closing.

"Hey, Giddy, where are—" Linus's words got instantly cut off as he came through the door and found a gun practically pressed to his nose.

Linus flailed for a moment, making a noise like a startled dolphin but quickly settled when Santos flashed him his FBI badge.

"What's this all about?" Linus asked, giving Gideon a pleading look as if Gideon had any ability to help him.

Quinn stepped up to Linus. "We just have a few questions, Mr. Hartley. As long as you answer honestly, you have nothing to worry about. Follow me, please."

Linus gave one last look to Gideon, looking like a kicked puppy, before following Quinn into the breakroom. Wiz announced that she would keep an eye out front for Mr. Peterson's arrival so everyone else could watch the interrogation.

Quinn had Linus sit in an office chair, then took a seat facing him. She looked over and met Gideon's eyes, giving him a smile like she was excited to show off for him.

"Mr. Hartley, may I call you Linus?" When Linus nodded, she continued, "I need you to stare directly into my eyes. Hold my gaze as best as you can. Can you do that?"

Linus nodded wordlessly, looking lost and dazed.

"Perfect. I want you to keep looking directly into my eyes and don't look away, okay? That's good," Quinn said, her voice soothing and low. "How long have you worked here at the crematorium?"

"Six years," Linus replied.

"What do you do here, Linus?"

Linus explained his job, his voice starting to sound sleepy and almost robotic.

"Good. Can you tell me the name of the owner?"

Gideon stepped closer and almost answered the question. Realizing what had happened, he shook his head, trying to break loose the hold Quinn's magic had taken on him. It was a quiet magic, soothing and lulling. Unlike everyone else's magic that he'd met so far, it was subtle. Now that he was paying attention, he could sense the tendrils of persuasion reaching out from

Quinn and wrapping around Linus. Gideon dug his fingernails into his palm, keeping himself grounded.

"Have you ever met an Officer Alan Kaminski or a Dr. Claude Leroux?"

"I don't know those names However, there is a police officer who visits sometimes. I think he's a friend of Mr. Peterson's but I don't know his name. They spend time in his office."

"You ever hear what they talk about?"

Linus shook his head, looking ready to cry, as if he was brokenhearted at letting Quinn down.

Gideon stood there, his senses tingling as he experienced the enchanting aura of her creeping, persuasive magic. It was unlike anything he had ever encountered before – a delicate balance of subtlety and power. The gentle waves of her magic washed over him, imbuing his thoughts with a strange sense of ease and trust. It felt as if a comforting hand was guiding him, urging him to reveal his deepest, darkest secrets.

He took a cautious step back, creating more distance between himself and Quinn. He knew better than to let himself be swayed entirely by the irresistible pull of her coercion.

As he glanced over at Dacey, he could see a flicker of acknowledgment in her eyes. She, too, was aware of the influence emanating from Quinn. Dacey's expression hardened, and she subtly positioned herself closer to Gideon, as if to provide a shield against the enchanting spell trying to worm its way into his subconscious.

Quinn asked Linus a bunch of questions regarding Mr. Peterson, the police officer he'd seen, and the crematorium. It became quickly apparent both that Linus was innocent of any criminal involvement and had no idea anything untoward was happening at his place of work.

"We can cut him loose. I doubt he's got anything else that can help us. Santos, can you switch with Wiz so she can get Mr. Hartley on his way?"

Santos dipped his chin and headed out of the room. A moment later, Wiz entered the room with a black bag slung over her shoulder. Gideon gave the bag a wary look and then glanced over at Dacey. "What happens now?" he whispered to her.

"Wiz will erase his memory of this entire event. She'll then send him home, making him believe that Mr. Peterson gave him the day off or that he got sent home because of malfunctioning equipment or something."

Gideon's eyes widened. He perked up, intrigued and disturbed at the thought of watching someone's memories get erased. Wiz retrieved a small cloth pouch from her bag and dipped her finger into it. When she set the pouch aside, Gideon noticed that the tip of her finger looked like she'd covered it in graphite shavings.

"Stay still," Wiz commanded Linus, who looked like he was starting to come out of the trance-like state Quinn had put him in. He started to open his mouth to protest, but Wiz pressed her finger to his forehead, cutting off his words.

The growing fear on Linus's face washed away at the first touch. Wiz pressed her finger gently, yet purposefully, onto Linus's forehead, the contact making him tremble for a moment before he went completely still. Wiz said some kind of foreign or nonsense word, and a surge of energy coursed out from where Wiz was touching Linus. His body went limp in the chair, like a marionette whose strings had been severed. Her lips moved in an almost silent incantation of unintelligible words, and Gideon felt the magic swirl out from where Wiz's finger was still pressed to Linus's skin.

Time seemed to momentarily pause as Gideon watched with bated breath.

"Hey, Linus, I need you to look into my eyes. That's right. Good job. Can you understand me?" Wiz asked, her voice firm yet soothing.

"Yes," Linus replied, his voice once again soft and robotic. Wiz removed her finger from Linus's forehead and curled her hands in her lap.

"Excellent. I am Mr. Peterson, your boss."

Linus nodded slowly, his head wobbling on his neck. "Mr. Peterson," he repeated.

"Okay, Linus. It's just you and me here in the crematorium. No one else is here but us. You're going to leave and head home. The ovens here needed to be unexpectedly serviced, so you're getting the day off. Can you repeat that for me?"

Linus repeated the words as Gideon shifted awkwardly on his feet. The magic emanating from the dark smear on Linus's forehead felt similar to Quinn's suggestive magic, except it was more like a gong than a subtle ringing of a bell. Gideon could almost feel a vacuum left in Linus's mind from his stolen memories and Wiz's magic washing in to fill it with her words. Gideon understood the necessity of what they were doing but was deeply uncomfortable with the ethics of messing with someone's mind and memories.

"That's perfect, Linus." Wiz reached into the bag and pulled out a napkin. "You are going to leave here and get in your car to head home. Once you get in your car, I want you to wipe away every trace of the smudge on your forehead. You got some dirt on it, and you want your face clean. Do you understand?"

When Linus nodded again, Wiz gave him a bright smile. "Alright, Linus. You can go home now."

As Wiz finished speaking, Linus stirred, his unfocused gaze sharpening once more. A flicker of confusion danced across his features, soon replaced by a resigned acceptance. "Okay, Mr. Peterson. I'll head home, but I expect to be paid for the day since I had to drive all this way."

Wiz nodded. "That's fair."

With stilted movements, Linus got up from his chair, took the offered napkin, and headed out. Following behind him, Gideon watched as he complained under his breath about a wasted journey – that Mr. Peterson could have saved him the drive if he'd just called beforehand and he could've slept in. Still muttering, Linus left through the front door and got into his truck. He sat for a minute, wiping his face before driving away.

When Wiz stepped up next to Gideon, watching with him as Linus's truck turned a corner and disappeared, he barely managed to keep from flinching away from the woman.

"That bothered you," Wiz murmured, not looking at Gideon.

"Yeah, it did. I don't like Linus much but watching someone mess with his mind felt invasive. He'll never know, I guess. But that means that this kind of thing could happen to anyone, and they'd never know. That is scary to me. It just doesn't seem right."

"I understand. There is no real harm with the magic itself. It causes no lasting damage. All Linus will be left with is a day off from work and, I imagine, a lingering annoyance that he had to come in when Mr. Peterson could have called him at home instead. I don't like erasing people's memories, but humans can't find out about us. The safety of all Mythicals is more important than a single person. We don't want another Spanish Inquisition. I wish that Mythicals could live in harmony with humans, but I don't trust them. So, if I occasionally must alter someone's memories to keep that from happening, then that's what I'll do. Linus will never know what happened here and although you might not believe me, that's a good thing. And as far as hurting someone and hiding it – Mythicals with my kind of abilities are closely monitored for this very reason."

Gideon wanted to live in a world where morality was black and white. Dacey and her magical co-workers seemed to live in shades of gray. To Gideon, messing with someone's memory was wrong. To the rest of them, it was just a necessary evil.

Suddenly, Gideon honestly wasn't sure he wanted any part of this anymore.

Just as he was about to turn away from the front door, he

spotted his boss's shiny Mercedes screeching into the parking lot. Mr. Peterson got out of his car and slammed the door.

Gideon called out a warning to the team as he stomped his way across the parking lot, his voice cutting through the silence. "Mr. Peterson is here."

Immediately, Santos took charge, his authoritative presence commanding everyone else to disperse and head to the back, instructing them to wait until further notice.

"Can you distract him as he comes inside?" Santos requested. "I want to ensure we catch him unguarded."

Gideon nodded, staring out the front window uncertainly as Mr. Peterson slid his key into the front door, his face a mask of irritation. He did a double take when he opened the door and found Gideon standing in the middle of the room, not noticing Santos off to the side.

"What are you doing out here? Why aren't you in the back? And why the hell did I just spot Linus driving away?" Mr. Peterson yelled, looking like he was building up a good head of steam.

Gideon's heart raced as he watched the confusion flash across Mr. Peterson's face when he finally noticed Santos standing off to the side.

"Wha—?" Mr. Peterson started to ask when Santos flashed his FBI badge, the gleaming emblem catching his boss's attention. The man stood, shocked and panting for a moment, before turning and trying to flee back out the front of the building. Desperation fueled his disheveled movements as he flailed with the doorknob. But before he could even get the door re-opened, Santos was swiftly across the room, seizing Mr. Peterson's arm with a firm grip. Santos shook the bewildered man.

"Where do you think you're going?" said Santos. "We have some questions for you, Mr. Peterson."

CHAPTER 22

Gideon stood silently in the records room with the rest of Dacey's crew, his gaze fixed on Quinn as she conducted the intense interrogation of Mr. Peterson. The atmosphere felt heavy and oppressive to Gideon, as if the truth itself hung in the air. He watched silently as Quinn hypnotized his boss, easily bending his will to her own, just like she'd done to Linus earlier.

"Are you picking up any magic from him?" Dacey whispered to Gideon, indicating Mr. Peterson.

Gideon pushed his senses out but shook his head when he didn't feel anything from his boss. He gave Dacey a one-shoulder shrug. "Feels human, I guess."

Dacey nodded before turning her attention back to Quinn's questioning.

It didn't take long for Peterson to succumb. The man's eyes darted nervously, his voice trembling as he confessed that three months ago, a police officer had caught him in a compromising position with a prostitute. Gideon felt nauseous as he listened to Mr. Peterson give excuse after excuse, trying to justify his behavior.

"My wife would've taken everything if she found out," Mr. Peterson whined pathetically. "When Kaminski told me he could get me out of it, I took his offer without question."

"What was his offer?" Quinn asked.

The insidious agreement was simple: Peterson merely needed to ensure that the paperwork provided by the officer went unquestioned. Moreover, whenever he received a body that had been sent to him from Kaminski and Leroux, he needed to ensure that the corpse didn't get viewed or the paperwork questioned.

"And you never questioned why he needed to dispose of these bodies?" Quinn asked.

"I—I, uh, assumed that it was, uh, vigilante justice or something," Mr. Peterson lamely stuttered out. At Quinn's raised eyebrow, he turned bright red. "I didn't *want* to know, okay? It was better for my long-term health to not ask any questions. I didn't want to end up in a box as well."

Gideon could see Quinn gritting her teeth, her throat convulsing, like she was physically having to swallow her anger. "Did you ever take a look at any of the bodies?"

Mr. Peterson gulped, looking guilty as hell, before nodding. "Um, I did once."

"Who was it?"

"It was a younger guy, maybe in his early twenties. His throat had been slashed open but the death certificate said he had an overdose. His name was Colin… something with a T, I think."

"Colin Thorpe?" Dacey quickly supplied.

"Yes, I think that was it."

Gideon decided that he'd heard enough. Turning on his heel, he stalked out of the room. He couldn't help but contemplate the depths of human depravity. Mr. Peterson was willing to overlook and cover up murders, just to hide his adultery from his wife. It was both shocking and not.

Without any forethought, he wandered into the viewing room

and took a seat in one of the pews. Resting his elbows on his knees, he stared at his clasped hands, trying to gather his scattered thoughts.

Someone sitting next to him jolted him. "Hey, Giddy. You okay?"

Gideon glanced over at Dacey and shrugged. "What happens now? I assume that Mr. Peterson is going to get arrested or something? And I'm going to lose this job?"

"I'm not sure what will happen with your job, but, yeah, Peterson is definitely going to jail."

Gideon knew that he was just feeling overwhelmed, but it was just one step too much. His job as a cremator had been a lifeline that kept him from drowning after the incident in college. Losing this job hurt. He and his mom were doing okay financially – they weren't struggling like they had when he was a kid – but they really couldn't afford for Gideon to lose his job. The shell shack didn't pay enough for them to keep up with their bills.

Now he was going to have to find a new job. Dacey had said he would make 'bank' as an auramancer, but after his conversation with Vena earlier, he knew that honing his magic skills would take time that he didn't have to spare. The rent wouldn't pay itself.

"If you guys don't need me here anymore, I think I'm going to head home," Gideon said. "I need to get ready for my shift at Sheryl's since I'm obviously losing this job. Honestly, I just want to have breakfast with my mom and forget this entire night."

Dacey bit her lip, looking almost guilty. "You can totally do that. But would you hang around for a bit longer? They're bringing in Leroux now and I just want you to confirm if you can sense that dark magic on him."

Gideon gritted his teeth but dipped his head in acquiescence.

Fifteen minutes later, movement out the window caught Gideon's attention. Three shiny black SUVs pulled into the parking lot. The last one into the lot maneuvered so it was parked across the entrance, blocking any traffic.

Dacey stood up and called out to the group. "Hey, guys, it looks like the Conclave agents are here."

MacGuire popped his head out the door leading to the restricted area a moment later. "Do we know if they picked up Kaminski too? Or is it just Leroux?"

Dacey shrugged and headed toward the locked front door. Gideon joined her, watching as all the doors on the SUVs opened and a squadron of people in sharp black suits swarmed out of the vehicles.

Amid the tightly knit cluster of people who resembled secret service agents stood a short, pot-bellied man clad in disheveled striped pajamas. His thinning brown hair tumbled messily around his face, indicating that he had been abruptly snatched from his slumber. His eyes darted nervously from one person to another, searching for any signs of friendliness or understanding. His hands, bound tightly in zip ties, trembled slightly. A bead of sweat trickled down his forehead and his breathing was shallow. He looked like he was seconds from passing out in fright. He didn't look like a cold-blooded killer to Gideon – not that he would know what one truly looked like.

Dacey unlocked the front door and waved everyone inside, re-locking it once the group had safely crossed the threshold.

As the group entered the room, the man's gaze remained lowered to the floor, his brow furrowed with worry. His face was red and splotchy like he'd been crying. He visibly flinched at every sound, as if bracing himself for an imminent strike.

"You don't have Kaminski in custody yet?" Dacey asked one of the agents.

A man, sporting a pair of dark aviator glasses, shook his head. "He wasn't home. We have people camped out on both ends of his street. We'll nab him as soon as he returns."

"Do you think he got tipped off?" Dacey asked.

The same agent shook his head. "No chance. We pulled this one straight from his bed. He never got a chance to send out a warning."

Gideon stared at the unassuming-looking man, struggling to reconcile the image with the heinous crimes he had committed. It seemed inconceivable. Yet, there he stood, the perpetrator of unspeakable crimes, looking like a lost and scared little lamb.

But as Leroux frog-marched further into the lobby, he came abreast of Gideon. A malevolent aura emanated from him, engulfing the room with its foul magic. Gideon instinctively recoiled, his senses assaulted by the darkness. A wave of revulsion washed over him, his thoughts momentarily clouded by a primordial instinct to run.

Taking a deep breath, Gideon slowly regained his composure. Dacey looked at him and raised an expectant eyebrow. "Well?" she asked.

Swallowing down his nausea, Gideon nodded. "It's the same magic. Although I thought it would be worse," Gideon responded, thinking of Leroux's house and how strong the magic felt there when the maid had opened the door. Perhaps he was getting used to it after repeated exposure. Or maybe it was because Leroux spent a lot of time in his home and it had seeped into the very foundation of the building, like the stench of someone stinky repeatedly sitting on a chair, each time magnifying the lingering, foul odor until it was unbearable.

Gideon glanced down at his watch and back up at Dacey. She gave him a knowing look. "You need to go?"

"Yeah, if you guys don't need me here for the rest of it, I'd like to go home. I need to shower and eat before I head to my other job."

"Hey, can I come with you? I'd love to say hi to your mom, and, frankly, I'm starving. Someone on the team will be happy to pick me up afterward, so you don't need to worry about giving me a ride back."

Gideon was tempted to say no, but in the end, he nodded. He knew that Dacey was worried about him, and he suspected that she was going to try to talk him into working for the magical organization that employed her – this Conclave or whatever. He wasn't ready to consider tying himself further into this magical world yet, but he'd let her pitch it to him. "I'll text Mom and let her know you're coming."

As he walked out the front door a few minutes later – after saying goodbye to the team – Gideon got in his car and took a moment to stare at the crematorium. It felt weird to admit – even just to himself – but he was going to miss the job.

CHAPTER 23

The sky transformed from the last lingering pinks and lavenders of twilight to clear and vibrant as Gideon drove home. On his left, the sun reflected off the gulf's water creating a sparkling vista. Occasional surfers dotted the waves like buoys floating in the ocean. He remembered that Zen once referred to the surfers who beat the sunrise to catch waves as the Dawn Patrol. They were out in droves, probably wanting to stake out their favorite surfing spot before the throng of usual early-season spring breakers made their way to the beaches.

In the midst of this breathtaking spectacle, Dacey sat beside Gideon as he drove, her voice filled with passion as she extolled the virtues of joining the Conclave. Her words were filled with conviction, painting an appealing image of incredible adventures. And money. Gideon listened, allowing her tempting words to wash over him like the waves on the beach just passing outside his car's window.

"How dangerous is your work?" he asked. "Because I can't regenerate like you."

"You could be a contractor, which is what I am, and then you could pick and choose the jobs you are willing to work. You don't have to take any of the dangerous assignments. You can work at your regular job and take on Conclave assignments when it suits you."

Gideon bit his lip, more tempted than he wanted to let on.

"Plus, the Conclave will train you to use your magic. They'll see the potential in you, just like they did with me. They'll fall all over themselves to get you to work with them, even as a contractor. You'd be a valuable asset. I guarantee that they'll be willing to provide whatever you need, including stuff like self-defense and anything else that would help you."

"Would I have to pay for training?"

"No way. They'd do that for free. Although they might put some stipulations on it – usually an NDA and a non-compete with other Conclaves. But you'd be able to negotiate the terms. Dude, with your abilities, I could really use your help on some of my gigs. We could work together, Gideon. You'd be saving me from being assigned to work with MacGuire, and you know how he gets on my nerves."

The wheedling tone made Gideon shake his head and hide a smile. "Let me think about it, okay?"

The sun climbed higher, reflecting so brightly off the water it hurt to look at the ocean. Gideon was lost in his head, considering Dacey's suggestion. He knew that this decision held immense weight, one that would reshape his future.

"I understand, I do. Just… seriously, think about it," Dacey suggested. "You're going to need to learn how to use your magic anyhow, so why not do it on the Conclave's dime?"

Gideon gave her a look out of the corner of his eye, keeping the bulk of his attention on the road. "I need time to process. The past few days have been a lot."

Dacey looked like she wanted to say more but nodded and fell silent, staring out of the window quietly watching the landscape pass by. She must've sensed that pushing Gideon further would backfire.

As Gideon's car rolled to a stop in front of the modest apartment building, Dacey cleared her throat. "I wanted to say thank you. You've been an amazing help on this case, and I've enjoyed working with you. You're a pretty good partner, Gideon Bean."

Gideon didn't know what to say, so he just awkwardly cleared his throat and bobbed his head in acknowledgment.

"Also, even if you decide against working with the Conclave, I know that Vena will happily give you guidance or recommend someone who can help you work on your skills. You should use her as a resource either way."

"I'll think about it," Gideon promised.

Turning off the car, Gideon sat for a moment, staring unseeingly at his apartment's front door.

"How much longer are you in town?" he asked.

Dacey made an unsure sound. "I'm not sure. Now that they have Peterson and Leroux, they'll be able to unravel this entire operation with ease. Unless they want my help bringing in any other suspects, I'll probably be sent home later today."

Gideon nodded at her words, confirming what he'd suspected.

"Well, let's go get some breakfast. And… you get to be the one to tell my mom you're leaving town." Gideon gave her a mock sad face. "You're gonna break her heart."

"Damn, you're cold, Giddy!" Dacey complained, laughter filling her voice as she got out of the car.

"Gideon," he corrected again.

"Mhm," was the only response from Dacey who grinned at him teasingly.

Walking up the tiny pathway to his front door, they bickered and teased one another like old friends. It felt natural and fun, and Gideon shoved away the tiny kernel of sadness at losing the camaraderie with Dacey so soon after meeting her. His life would never feel the same – in both a good and a bad way.

Despite it still being early morning, the heat of the day was already growing unbearable. Getting ready to unlock the door, Gideon wiped the sweat from his brow with his sleeve. "Ugh," he complained. "I can still feel Leroux's magic clinging to me, I swear. I need a shower so bad. Or maybe some bleach."

Dacey wrinkled her nose in commiseration. "So glad I can't feel it. I don't envy you. Yuck-o."

Gideon unlocked his door and started to swing it open, calling out a greeting to his mom. The words choked and got stuck in his throat when a dark familiar magic washed over him from inside his apartment.

"*Mom*—" he started to scream when he felt a sudden impact, a ball of clear liquid hitting and breaking open against his chest, splashing against him like a tossed water balloon. Whatever the liquid was, it felt like a punch to his face. Gasping, Gideon dropped to his knees, clinging weakly to the doorknob as he started to lose his grasp on consciousness.

A flare of fire bloomed behind him, lighting up the living room and revealing two men. His mom was lying on the floor at the men's feet. He panicked, his voice breaking over a garbled scream, because he couldn't tell if she was okay or not. Another clear ball sailed out of the room and over his head. He realized it hit Dacey because the orange glow of her fire went out like it had been doused in a bucket of water. He heard the thump of her body hitting the ground behind him.

As he tried to hold onto the last vestiges of his consciousness, the familiar foul, malevolent magic encased him in its chilling embrace. His breath was slowing, but his heart raced with fear and his palms were clammy, making his grip on the doorknob slip. Before he could even absorb the situation or respond, Gideon's grip faltered, and he tumbled down to the floor.

As his eyelids grew heavier, threatening to seal shut, he caught a glimpse of a figure approaching through the haze. It was a beefy blond man in the uniform of a police officer. A malicious sneer etched across his face, confirming Gideon's worst fears. Another man appeared next to him. This man was dressed like he was ready for a day on the golf course, with a mint green polo shirt tucked into tan khaki pants.

The force of strange liquid magic spreading across his chest was overwhelming, causing his breath to catch in his throat as his consciousness wavered on the precipice. Desperately, he managed to utter a single word, "Mom."

CHAPTER 24

Something awoke Gideon. Opening his bleary eyes, he found himself flat on his back, gazing up at a dense canopy of trees that formed a natural cover overhead. He also thought he smelled a campfire, his sluggish brain confused and slow-moving. An annoying, buzzing mosquito landed on his cheek and bit him. He tried to swat it away, but his hand wouldn't move from where it was resting at his side. Fear washed away Gideon's groggy state, replacing it with rising confusion and dread. Alarm surged through his veins as he tried to move his limbs, only to find himself numb and immobilized. His vision went fuzzy from panic, as he struggled to make sense of his paralyzed body and remember why he was outside, lying on the forest floor.

Straining his senses, Gideon heard hushed voices conversing nearby; the pounding of his pulse made it impossible to make out any words. He tried to slow and quiet his breathing, needing to listen, but horror and sick anticipation made it almost impossible.

His memories crashed back like a torrential wave, the recollection of the two men who had ambushed him and Dacey at his mom's apartment returning in a wave. As he remembered how they had rendered him unconscious, Gideon had to grit his teeth to refrain from making any noise. He could still feel the liquid drenching his shirt. The magic of it felt like a sticky, void-like blank that was still clinging to his torso, trying to pull him back into slumber.

The feeling of it on his skin was almost drowned out by the dense, malevolent magic that enveloped the atmosphere around him. The very air he was breathing was saturated with a noxious miasma, clouding his senses. He tried to push out his auramancer powers to make sense of what he was experiencing, but he was swamped by the thick, sickly magic flooding the area.

"This sucks. I liked being a police officer. I don't want to swap bodies again," a male voice complained.

With great effort, Gideon finally managed to slowly turn his head minutely, trying to locate the source of the voices.

"Well, you're the imbecile that just had to keep snatching college kids. I told you to stick to the homeless, but you just wanted to punish rich kids. You brought too much attention down on us."

"I know, it's just that they're so…. Whatever, it doesn't matter now. We'll stick to the homeless and the elderly from now on," the first voice promised. "We're so close. It will only take maybe a dozen more."

"Yes, but we still need to be able to source the sacrifices and you can't use that body anymore. What's the plan now?"

"Well, we know they're onto me since my surveillance cameras caught these two prowling around my house. So, I need a new body, and, obviously, Azzernon needs a new one too. Let's sacrifice the woman, then I will take possession of the man's body and Azzernon can have the mom's. Once we make the swap, and I'm out of this body, we can kill Kaminski as well. I say we stage it as if Kaminski killed the girl, and the new guy fought him off and killed the police officer, saving himself and his mom.

Having him working at the crematorium will be convenient for future disposals, so losing Leroux won't be so bad."

"What about my body? Do I need to get a new one too?" the second voice asked.

"No one's been sniffing around the golf course, so I think you're safe for now. We'll lay low for a week or two. If anyone comes after you, just abandon the body and we'll find you a new one."

Straining every muscle, Gideon finally turned his head enough to spot a man dressed in a police uniform. He assumed that he was looking at Alan Kaminski. The other man, in the golfing outfit, came into view, grunting and dragging something behind him. Gideon froze his efforts to wake up his unmovable limbs and closed his eyes to slits.

Through his narrowed vision, he watched the man drag his mom's unconscious body across the ground and dump her at Gideon's side. Once the man turned his back, Gideon opened his eyes and stared at his mom. Relief swamped Gideon when he saw her chest rise and fall.

Gideon turned his attention back to the golfer and watched as he returned to Kaminski's side. Both men leaned over a prone form. Gideon managed to keep silent when he realized that they were looming over Dacey.

"She looks just like that woman we sacrificed the other day."

"Huh? Which one?"

"You know. You said you spotted a drunk woman wandering all alone down John Sims Parkway and it was a convenient grab. Then when you were taking her to the car, some guy attacked you. You thought it was her father or something."

"Oh, yeah. She does look like that girl. Probably her sister or something." Kaminski shrugged like he didn't care.

"Okay, maybe. But why was she with the guy who works at the crematorium? Don't you find that a little suspicious?"

"Must you always be such a worrier, Vormak? This is fine. It doesn't matter. Once I take over his body, I'll have access to his memories, and we'll be able to figure this all out. Then, we'll find out if anyone else suspects what's going on. If it all goes to shit, we'll just get new bodies."

Gideon's heart pounded. What the hell was going on and what was he going to do to stop it? At least he wasn't tied up – if only he could move his damn arms and legs. His mind raced with a mix of fear and determination.

Gideon had to remind himself to keep his eyes mostly closed as he watched Kaminski walk over to a massive cauldron made of blackened iron. Its presence in the middle of the woods was so strange that Gideon didn't know what to make of it. It sat, like a fat squat spider over a campfire with steam rising from its interior. The vessel was large enough to fit a body inside its belly, and its height nearly reached the cop's thigh. The cauldron seemed ancient, adorned with intricate engravings and fire-blackened sides.

The two men, standing sideways to Gideon so he could see both their faces, gathered around the cauldron. The golfer, who must be Vormak, took a small ziplock out of a pocket and tore it open, revealing a powdery substance. He poured its contents into the cauldron, causing a vibrant blue plume of smoke to rise from the concoction. Along with the mushroom cloud of smoke, a bizarre magic issued from the cauldron's depths. It felt like searing heat and icy suffocating weight at the same time. Combined with the sickly dark magic emanating from his captors, it made Gideon's gorge rise. He took small shallow breaths, trying to keep the contents of his stomach in place. A vision of throwing up while paralyzed filled him with terrifying ideas of choking to death on his own vomit.

Gideon realized that most of the dark magic filling the area wasn't just originating from the two men, but from an area in the forest just a few feet past the cauldron. His gaze fixated on a scorched area on the ground, where the grass had been seared away, leaving behind an eerie blackened circle.

Using a long stick, Vormak vigorously stirred the mixture, the swirling liquid emitted an otherworldly glow.

"Is it ready?" Kaminski asked, dusting his hands off on his police-issued pants.

Vormak leaned over the contents of the cauldron, unfazed by any heat rising from its bubbling brew – his face twisted in anticipation – and inhaled deeply. A pleased expression crossed his features.

"Almost. Once we finish sacrificing the girl, we'll be ready to get you into your new body."

The golfer stopped and looked over his shoulder and made a face at the empty air behind him. "No, you get to wait, asshole. You're the one who didn't even realize that people were breaking into your fancy house. We had an escape plan and you fucked it up. An expensive alarm system, and you didn't even set it before you went to bed."

Vormak stopped and stared silently into the empty air before scoffing angrily. "I don't give a shit. You get the woman's body. I'm not going to argue with you anymore. If you hate it that much, we can get you a different conduit later. Stop bitchin', because you're slowing us down for no reason."

A thought occurred to Gideon that maybe Vormak wasn't talking to thin air – maybe there was someone else there who was invisible. He could hardly believe what he was witnessing.

Gideon pushed his awareness through the malevolent energy-charged air around him, directing it toward the two men. Opening his senses like he'd been practicing, he realized that he could feel three individual sources of dark magic, along with the strange sickening aura emitting from the dark scorched circle in the earth.

These men kept discussing swapping bodies. Could this invisible apparition be a ghost that had been possessing Leroux's body? Was that why Leroux had seemed so lost and confused when they brought him into the crematorium this morning? Because he didn't know his body had been used to commit and/or hide murders? Maybe that's why the dark magic rising from Leroux's body didn't feel as strong as Gideon thought it should have – because the true source of the foul miasma had abandoned its vessel. The thought sent a shiver down Gideon's spine.

Feeling like he was running out of time, Gideon strained his useless limbs, desperately attempting to regain control of his muscles. When he was able to finally wiggle his toes, hope blossomed in his chest, then immediately faltered as he watched the two men roughly yank Dacey's unconscious body off the ground. She hung limp between the two men, as they dragged her over to the edge of the burnt grass.

Vormak propped Dacey up on her knees, holding her by her shoulders to keep her from falling over as Kaminski stepped away. Her head hung lifelessly between her shoulders, her features obscured by a curtain of disheveled hair.

With an anticipatory grin, Kaminski picked something off the ground near the cauldron. Gideon's breath caught when he realized that the police officer was gripping an ornate, bejeweled knife. As he approached Dacey, Gideon's fear transformed into a fierce surge of adrenaline. He redoubled his efforts, his mind consumed by a singular thought: to save Dacey from a gruesome death.

CHAPTER 25

Dread and panic surged through Gideon, his breaths rapid and unsteady. His gaze fixed on the man holding a knife to Dacey's throat, lifting her head forcefully by her hair. Desperation coursed through Gideon's veins as he fought to gain command over his paralyzed limbs. With a quiet grunt, he mustered every ounce of strength, finally coaxing his limbs to twitch in response. But they proved uncooperative, flopping uselessly on the ground like a fish out of water. The sound of his efforts caused Kaminski to pause, the knife pressed against Dacey's throat. A small trail of blood trickled down Dacey's neck. The man straightened and glanced in Gideon's direction. Gideon froze, pretending to still be unconscious.

"What was that?" Vormak blurted, his voice strung tight with anxiety.

"I don't know," the other man replied, seeming less worried. "Let me go check."

As Kaminski approached, knife still in hand, Gideon closed his eyes, playing possum. Sensing the man looming over him and his mother, Gideon listened intently, the shade created by the man's body letting Gideon know that he was right above him, studying their motionless forms. Gideon kept his face blank and serene, channeling his focus into wiggling his toes within his shoes, determined to rouse his dormant body. When he heard the man turn and start walking away; he seized the opportunity and tried to launch himself off the ground, to strike at the man's back, but his body failed him again, floundering uselessly.

Now that the ruse was over, Gideon opened his eyes and watched helplessly as Kaminski ran back and delivered a swift kick to his side. Gideon groaned loudly as pain surged through him. Agony radiated through his body, but he refused to succumb to the siren call of unconsciousness.

When Kaminski loomed near, Gideon closed his eyes again, not wanting to see what happened next. A thumb was pressed beneath one of his eyes and his eyelid was forcibly pried open. Gideon was met with the sneering face of Kaminski.

"Looks like this one is starting to wake up. You must not have gotten enough of the knock-out spell on him, Vormak," Kaminski jeered.

The other man sniffed as if put out. "Well, let's not waste any more time. We'll deal with him next. He won't be able to move for quite a while, so let's just get this done. I need to be back at the pro shop in two hours."

When Kaminski finally released his face, all that met Gideon's gaze was the darkness of the back of his eyelid. As he listened to Kaminski striding away, he mustered the strength to slowly open his eyes once more.

His heart hadn't stopped pounding since the moment he regained consciousness, but now it intensified, the fear and desperation coursing through his veins like a poison as he watched Kaminski stride back toward Dacey.

"Stop! Please!" he shouted when Kaminski placed the knife against her throat again. The blond officer looked up and caught Gideon's eyes, giving him a wide teeth-filled smile as he sliced the knife across Dacey's throat in a quick slashing motion.

Gideon shouted as Dacey's blood fountained and soaked the scorched earth at her knees. His sight blurred and his throat burned as he yelled. He flopped on the ground, much like an elephant seal trying to maneuver on land, desperately trying to reach her.

Through blurry vision, Gideon watched as Dacey's blood splashed onto the scorched earth. When the blood reached the ground, a surge of malevolent magic erupted from the blackened earth, engulfing and burning out Gideon's senses. Crimson tendrils of magic reached towards the sky, a manifestation of deadly power that sent terror skittering down Gideon's spine. The blast of red-hot magic shot up from the burnt ground like a volcano erupting. The magic felt like burning necrotic death. It made Gideon think of witches being burned at the stake or sacrifice victims being consumed by lava. The intensity of the magic made Gideon retch. Tears leaked from his burning, blinded eyes.

With fury coursing through his veins, he screamed at the two men, bellowing about how he would kill them both if it was the last thing he did.

Kaminski and Vormak's laughter at Gideon's threats echoed around the clearing. But Gideon couldn't care less about their taunts. His vision was slowly returning, and he couldn't look away from Dacey's slumped form, lying splayed on the ground where they'd dropped her on the edge of the circle.

After only a few minutes, Dacey's blood finally stopped flowing and the two men tossed her body aside like unwanted garbage. Gideon had seen hundreds of dead bodies, but he'd never actually witnessed death before. Even though he understood that Dacey could be resurrected, it was a horror that would haunt him for the rest of his days – however many of those he had left.

Panic gripped him when Kaminski directed his chilling gaze towards him, stalking purposefully in his direction. Knowing that this asshole wanted to possess his body made hot panic race through his nervous system. Death seemed preferable.

Remembering the zippo lighter in his pocket that Dacey had given him only two days ago, hope flared in Gideon's chest. If he could somehow set Dacey on fire, she would regenerate and escape.

Kaminski grabbed Gideon's ankle in an iron grip, dragging him across the unforgiving terrain. Rocks and sticks poked and scraped along Gideon's back, but it was the least of his concerns. His only focus was on trying to get his hand into his pocket, and on the lighter inside it. Desperation fueled his movements. The world was a blur around him, pain and foul magic making it impossible to focus his eyes. He managed to inch his hand to the pocket of his jeans but couldn't make his fingers cooperate enough to force them around the lighter.

As Kaminski dragged him past Dacey's slumped and still body, Gideon threw his free hand out and grasped her shirt, twisting his hand into the fabric. Kaminski tugged on him, shaking him, and trying to loosen Gideon's grip on Dacey's clothing. The cotton of her shirt made ripping sounds but held firm.

"Let her go, you idiot. She's dead, just like you'll be if you don't release her," Kaminski growled.

"Please," Gideon begged. "Just let me say goodbye."

Vormak made an annoyed, frustrated sound, but Kaminski chuckled in an indulgent way that made Gideon want to ram a stick through his eye. "Aww, Vormak, isn't he sweet? He wants to say goodbye to his girlfriend. I love it when humans cry."

Then the asshole dumped Gideon directly on top of Dacey's still, silent body. Gideon knew it was only his overactive imagination, but he could swear that she was already getting cold and stiff. The hand Gideon had managed to partially worm into his pocket was now trapped between his body and Dacey's.

As Gideon struggled to free himself, he became acutely aware of a dampness seeping into his clothes, soaking through the fabric into his skin. Looking down, he saw that he was drenched in a visceral, vibrant red. Dacey's blood, fresh and hot, clung to him like a ghastly shroud. The coppery smell of iron quickly filled his nostrils and left a metallic taste in his mouth. Horror welled up in his gut as he slid in the slippery, wet stickiness.

Gideon reared back as far as he could so that he could look at Dacey's face. Her skin was waxy and washed out from blood loss, but he would have thought she was only asleep otherwise.

They were lying in a small grassy area between the scorched circle where Dacey's blood had been sprayed and the cauldron. The crackling flames of the campfire danced close enough that its heat was almost blisteringly hot against his side. Sweat trickled down his brow, mixing with the tears that streamed from his eyes.

In that moment, as despair almost consumed him, a wild and insane idea took hold of Gideon. Without giving himself time to doubt or rethink, he wrapped his free arm tightly around Dacey's shoulders and with all the strength in his body, rolled them both towards the blazing campfire.

CHAPTER 26

Pain seared through his body. As he rolled them both into the fire, Gideon knocked into the cauldron. Whatever burning liquid was inside the heavy pot splashed over his back, making him scream. Yet, strangely, a bittersweet sense of relief washed over him. The flames would devour everything – his grief, his guilt, his worry. In that blazing inferno, Gideon felt a flicker of freedom. His mind was strangely removed from what was happening to his body. Through the crackling sizzle of burning flesh and his own screams filling his ears, he could hear Kaminski and Vormak shouting. He knew that no matter what happened next, they wouldn't be able to use his body for their nefarious plans. He couldn't help but grin at that.

A subsonic boom seemed to shatter the very air around him. Gideon was flung off Dacey's body and straight into the air. With a sickening crunch, his momentum was cut short by a thick tree trunk. Like a discarded toy, Gideon crashed to the ground, the world spinning and dipping out of focus. Agony, unlike anything he'd ever experienced, racked every inch of his body. Waves of excruciating pain rippled through his entire being, but it was his back and shoulder that cried out the loudest.

Gideon was lost in a pain-induced haze when a piercing screech echoed through the air, jolting him back to awareness. He hadn't even realized that he had been losing consciousness. Summoning every ounce of strength and resolve he had left, he managed to roll over onto his battered front, then painstakingly raised himself onto trembling knees. His vision danced and wavered, turning into a long, dark tunnel for a long moment, but he persisted, determined to stop Kaminski and Vormak no matter what kind of pain he was in.

Absolute elation flooded his veins as his gaze landed on Dacey, her fiery wings unfurled, like a blazing sun, illuminating the entire forest around them in hues of brilliant yellows and oranges. Most of her clothes were burned away, just a few charred wisps still clinging to her frame. Despite that, she looked like an avenging angel sent to purge the world of evil. The fire within her eyes blazed bright with a righteous fury as if they held the power to banish darkness itself. It made Gideon's heart soar to see her alive and whole.

In her grasp was Kaminski, flailing and screaming in agony, the sound almost inhuman. She held him one-handed by his neck. His fingers scratched and scrabbled at her hand, trying to pry her loose. He writhed and shrieked as his body was engulfed in scorching flames. A small part of Gideon wanted to look away from the horror, but he needed to see Kaminski defeated with his own eyes. It took mere moments before the anguished screams were silenced and the evil of his magical aura evaporated. Once done, Dacey released the charred husk of his body, carelessly discarding it beside Vormak's already incinerated carcass.

Dacey looked down at the bodies dispassionately before turning and spotting Gideon across the clearing. The enraged look on her face morphed into one of shock and horror. "Oh my god, Giddy."

She started to run toward him when he felt a familiar dark magic sweeping past him. Instinctually, he knew it was the ghostly entity that had occupied Leroux's body, trying to escape. Without another thought, he lunged, grasping for the evil essence.

To his absolute shock, he grabbed ahold of the ghost in his mostly uninjured hand and held on. It tried to escape, wiggling and thrashing in his grip. It dragged him along the ground, his knees bumping and scraping along the brush-covered ground. Gideon, his face contorted in pain, desperately clung onto the unseen force. With every fiber of his being, he held on, his fingers digging into the substance of the ethereal being. But the entity was relentless, fighting and writhing to escape like a rabbit in a snare, and Gideon could feel his strength waning.

Summoning all his resolve, Gideon managed to reach out with his injured arm, his face contorting further as a wave of searing agony surged through him. Scrabbling around for anything that could help, he snatched hold of a small, low-hanging tree branch as he was dragged past it. The rough bark tore into his bloodied, burned palm.

His anguished screams pierced the air, reverberating across the desolate landscape. The pain in his left shoulder and hand was unbearable, an inferno that threatened to consume him entirely. It resonated so intensely within him that his own cries deafened his ears, leaving them ringing with a disorienting buzz.

Dacey rushed over, her eyes wide with fear and confusion.

"What's happening, Gideon? Are you alright?" she bellowed, her voice frantic and desperate.

"Kill it! Kill it!" Gideon screamed. "I've got a hold of it. Kill it!"

"What? What are you talking about?"

"I've got a hold on it. Burn it!" he screeched in Dacey's terrified face. He was in too much pain to form a coherent explanation, grunting with effort just to keep his hold on the insubstantial creature.

The confusion cleared off her face and with a determined look, she took a leap of faith and plunged her hand into the air over Gideon's straining grasp. Gideon gritted his teeth, pushing every ounce of his magic into the intangible monster, giving it substance.

Dacey gasped, her eyes wide and shocked. "I can feel it."

"Light it up!" Gideon commanded, sweat pouring down his face from the struggle.

"I don't want to burn your hands," Dacey cried. "Just let it go."

"No, you've got to kill it." When Dacey shook her head, Gideon firmed his voice. "Burn it. NOW!"

An unearthly, piercing howl reverberated through the air, sending shivers down his spine as Dacey's hands began to glow like molten lava. Gideon clenched his jaw, pouring every ounce of his power to keep the ghost materialized as heat from her fire burned his hand. A symphony of anguished wails and shrieks filled the air, from both the ghost and Gideon. It struggled relentlessly as Dacey's hands burst fully into flames inside the creature's incorporeal body. As she engulfed it in fire, its spectral form was revealed for a fleeting moment: a massive creature with horns, wings, and legs that bent the wrong way. Before Gideon could make sense of the monster's form, it emitted a tortured bellow as it succumbed to the relentless flames of Dacey's fire. She reduced it to mere ashes as if it were no more than a wispy piece of tissue paper. The ashes were quickly carried away by a gentle breeze that whispered through the forest clearing.

Exhausted and completely drained, Gideon collapsed, his eyelids heavy, fighting to maintain consciousness. Just as he was succumbing to the darkness, he felt Dacey's grip clasping onto him, trying to hold him upright before everything faded away.

Dacey's voice, loud and strident, woke Gideon up from the dark void of slumber. Dacey, who had always seemed cool and in charge, sounded completely freaked out. It had Gideon trying to surge to his feet, ready for battle, before he was completely awake. Adrenaline pumped through his veins, kicking his body into action.

Gideon made it up onto his knees before searing pain ripped through him, stopping his momentum. He made a noise like a dying whale, almost blacking out again. Each movement sent jolts of agony coursing through his entire body. He reached with his less injured hand instinctively, trying to touch his chest, something crunching and grinding in his upper left pec with each panicked breath. The intense pain caused Gideon to emit a desperate groan.

"Giddy? Oh my god, Giddy! Don't move okay, honey?" Gideon's mother's voice cut through the haze.

"Mom?" Gideon whispered, opening his eyes from where he was slumped, his head almost touching his knees on the forest floor. He hadn't noticed that his eyes had slid shut again. He was having trouble forming thoughts. Looking to the side, he found his mom, who looked almost as out of it as he felt, hovering next to him with both hands out like she wanted to grab him but couldn't figure out where she could touch that wouldn't hurt.

"Don't move, Gideon. You are seriously injured. Dacey's getting help. Do you understand, honey?"

Gideon nodded, his neck wobbly. "Yeah, Mom. I think I broke my collarbone," he said inanely, his words slurred and mumbling. Glancing down, he saw that both of his hands were bright red with large white blisters already forming on his skin. He had to look away because it somehow made the pain worse to stare at the oozing wounds.

"Hey, Ma," Gideon slurred. "Are you okay? Did those guys hurt you?"

His mom started crying in earnest at his question. "I'm fine. I'm not injured, I promise. But you're—"

Dacey's strident voice pulled his focus away from his mom. Gazing towards the sound of her voice, he spotted Dacey frantically pacing around the clearing, her voice filled with urgency as she spoke into a cell phone. "I don't care what you have to do," she yelled desperately. "He needs immediate medical attention. He needs to be air-lifted. Set it up – I don't care what it takes. Do it!"

As Dacey turned around in her agitated pacing, her eyes fell upon Gideon, who had somehow managed to find the strength to stay awake, despite the feeling that his body was trying to shut down on him again. She rushed towards him, dropping down to her knees in front of him.

"Gideon, are you okay?" Dacey's voice trembled, her eyes welling up with tears. "Don't move. You're covered in burns. They're sending a helicopter. We're going to get you to a healer in Tallahassee who can fix your injuries, okay? Just hang in there. We're going to get you all fixed up."

"Something's wrong with my shoulder. I think I broke my collarbone," he replied, his voice rasping and weak.

As she repeated the words to whoever was on the phone, Gideon was taken aback by the sight of tears streaming down her cheeks. It was a testament to the severity of his condition, but Gideon was just thankful they were all alive.

Gideon didn't like seeing Dacey cry. She was the toughest person he'd ever met.

"Hey, Dace," Gideon whispered. He waited until she leaned close to hear him better to ask, *"Are we having fun yet?"*

"Oh my god! That's not funny, Giddy." However, her sputtering, watery laugh said otherwise. "Just hang on, you jerk. We're gonna get you air-lifted out of here soon, okay?"

Gideon didn't think it took very long for the helicopter to arrive. However, time was moving in strange jolts and bursts. His mother's whispered prayers blended into a bizarre confusing reality. The sound of helicopter blades approaching brought fervent whispers of thanks from his mom.

As the helicopter hovered over the clearing, Gideon was

starting to lose the fight to stay conscious. The buzz of its blades filled the air, drowning out all other noise. Finally, the chopper found an optimal spot to touch down, its powerful gusts of wind rustling the trees into a frenzy. His weakened body trembled as he watched it slowly land, winds whipping through the glade, making him squint.

A group of paramedics swiftly piled out of the helicopter, their eyes focused and determined. They rushed towards Gideon, their faces professionally blank, but Gideon sensed both their urgency and compassion. They carefully positioned a stretcher beside him, its metal frame gleaming in the sunlight. Gideon groaned loudly as gentle hands skillfully secured him to the stretcher. They pushed the gurney back to the waiting helicopter, making Gideon wince with each bump and jostle across the clearing. They efficiently rolled him into the helicopter, locking his stretcher into place.

Through the haze of pain and exhaustion, Gideon's gaze shifted to his less burned arm. He watched as one of the paramedics deftly inserted an intravenous line into his vein. Gradually succumbing to the weight of weariness, Gideon glimpsed the paramedic's kind eyes, their warm expression offering him some solace. "We gotcha the good stuff. It's nightie-night time. You can relax. You're in good hands now," the paramedic whispered softly, a soothing lullaby that eased Gideon towards the waiting embrace of unconsciousness.

Right before he went entirely under, he heard Dacey's voice. He strained, trying to hear her.

"Nope. I'm pulling rank. I'm coming too. We both are," she declared fiercely, making Gideon grin as he fell asleep.

CHAPTER 27

Gideon woke up in an unfamiliar place.

His senses came online one by one, like a slowly booting computer. First, his sight returned. He stared blankly at an unfamiliar ceiling, his vision going in and out like a strobe light in a tunnel. Gideon's brain was so foggy he couldn't figure out what he was seeing. He wasn't sure how long he lay there, staring uncomprehendingly at the boring white ceiling above him. Next, feeling returned to his numbed body. He felt the cool unfamiliarity of clean sheets against his skin, the slight discomfort of a hard bed mattress under his sore body. His thoughts skittered away from his sense of touch – something teasing on the edge of his memory that made him switch his focus elsewhere. Thankfully, his sense of smell came online, distracting him. The scent in the air was strange: sterile, with a sharp, chemical tinge, underscored by a hint of a nauseating mixture of something sickly sweet and metallic. Whatever the smell was, Gideon's subconscious recoiled from it and veered back toward trying to analyze his surroundings.

His thoughts pinged and bounced around the inside of his skull like marbles in a shaken jar. His mind dipped and wove in and out of the fog of unconsciousness. Finally, sound made its way into his awareness. There was a soft, rhythmic beep off to his left, a muffled conversation in the distance, and the distinct sound of shoes on a hard floor.

"Welcome back," a feminine voice said, making his heavy head swivel on his neck towards it.

He found a woman of an indeterminate age with a stethoscope standing at his bedside. In a distant part of his slow-moving brain, he knew that he was in a hospital, so he sort of knew what to expect.

He tried to speak but was so dried out that all he could muster was a dusty croak.

A sympathetic tut escaped the woman's lips as she swiftly poured him a glass of water, filling it almost to the brim. Nodding gratefully, Gideon attempted to reach out for the cup, only to realize that his hands were wrapped in thick white bandages. He looked like he was wearing giant mittens. Thankfully, the woman held the cup to his lips, allowing him to take a much-needed sip of the refreshing liquid.

As Gideon finished his drink, he cleared his throat and asked, "Who are you?"

As he allowed himself to truly see her, he was caught off guard. The edges of her figure seemed to shimmer, a soft green glow seeping from her skin. It was like mist rising from a cold lake at dawn – ethereal and beautiful. The second surprise hit him when she placed one of her hands on his forehead and a wave of cool relief cascaded over him. It was as if a soothing ice pack had been placed on his fevered forehead. The woman's aura felt like an oasis in the desert, providing a comfort he didn't expect. An inexplicable sense of calm washed over him, slowing his racing thoughts, and dulling the edge of his anxiety and pain. Gideon briefly pondered if he was hallucinating.

"I'm Healer Airmid. I've been working on your burns and injuries."

"Where am I?" He instinctively knew he wasn't at his local hospital. He'd been there twice previously and was familiar with its pastel mauve color scheme.

The woman said the name of a hospital that Gideon had never heard of. At his blank look, the woman flashed him an amused smile. "Do you remember what happened?"

"Yeah, I—" Gideon started to answer, but then realized that he didn't know if he could divulge the information he had. He didn't think this woman was entirely human, but until he was certain, he knew he had to stay silent. Instead, he asked, "Um, my mother and my friend were with me, I think. Are they here?"

"Yes, they've been with you, by your side, since you arrived. But once we got you out of critical condition, investigators from the Conclave insisted that they both needed to be interviewed immediately. I thought your mother and Miss Menet were about to start swinging when the investigators told them they needed to leave your side," Healer Airmid said with a grin. "They both care about you a great deal. The only way I got them to go with the agents without a full-out brawl was by telling them that your rest couldn't be disturbed by a fight. However, since you're awake, I think they deserve to know. The investigators will just have to deal. I've been warned that we are keeping your mother in the dark as far as knowing that this is a Conclave facility. As far as she knows, everyone here is human and we're healing you with traditional human medicine."

As Gideon's mouth gaped open, trying to imagine his sweet mother attempting to punch someone and just not being able to picture it. The healer stepped towards the door like she was going to go find them.

"Wait, how long have I been here?"

The healer turned back and glanced at her watch that her sleeves had previously hidden. "Hmm, I think about six or seven hours, perhaps?"

Gideon sat there with his mouth opening and closing like a fish as the healer stepped quietly out of the room.

The door swung shut behind her, leaving Gideon alone with his spiraling thoughts. He wanted to get up and look in a mirror but was too terrified about what he might see. He weirdly didn't feel as much pain as he would've expected, though his entire body felt like one giant bruise and his skin was getting increasingly itchy now that he was paying attention to it. He'd once heard that serious burns were horrifically painful, so he couldn't figure out why he wasn't in agony. Perhaps he was just heavily drugged. Then he remembered hearing once that a person could damage their nerve endings so severely that they might temporarily lose sensation. The thought made a cold kind of terror bubble under his ribs.

A few minutes passed in silence while Gideon tried to contain his growing panic until his ears finally caught the stampede of approaching footsteps, growing thunderous. Suddenly, the door swung open, and his mother and Dacey rushed into the room, their faces a mix of panic and relief. Babbling in a frenzy, their voices overlapping, each one asking if he was alright.

Gideon held up his wrapped hands, urging them to quiet down. They both went instantly silent, both women staring at his bandaged hands mournfully.

"I'm fine. I surprisingly don't feel that bad." Gideon tried to assure them, although they didn't seem convinced. He felt guilty that they were so upset. And he wasn't totally lying. Granted – he felt like a bag of hammered shit, but he should have felt much, much worse. He was honestly more than a little surprised to still be alive.

Despite being burned to a crisp and thrown into a tree, he was somehow still breathing. He should have been writhing in unbearable torment or getting prepped to go into a retort oven. "Shouldn't I feel worse?" he finally asked.

His mother's eyes were knitted together in a mixture of relief and worry. A shaky sigh of relief tumbled out of her lips. "Do you know where you are, Giddy?"

She raised her hand, but wavered, seemingly unsure where to touch him without exacerbating his injuries. He caught her hand between his two wrapped hands. "Yeah, I'm in the hospital."

A tender smile crossed her face as she brushed a stray lock of hair from his forehead. "This isn't just some hospital, Gideon. This is the McAllen Burn Center. I've been told that it's one of the top places in the entire country for treating burns. They've got the best burn doctors here," she continued.

His mother nodded, a mixture of pride and concern painting her expression. "The doctor says that the burns aren't nearly as bad as they first appeared, and they should be able to heal with minimal scarring."

Gideon nodded, letting her comforting words sink in. The faint worry in his mother's tone did nothing to ease his own fears, but the very fact that he was in one of the best hands in the nation offered him a sliver of solace.

Gideon felt bad as he watched tears track down his mom's cheeks. "Aw, don't cry, Ma. I'm okay."

"I've never been so scared in my entire life. Don't you *ever* do that to me again!" Her eyes welled up with more tears, cascading down her face, at odds with the ferocious look she was giving him.

"I won't, Ma, I promise." Gideon would say anything to stop his mother's tears. Although, it was a promise he planned to keep.

"At least you didn't burn your handsome face," his mother said, pinching his cheek and making Gideon roll his eyes although he silently agreed. Burning his face would've sucked.

Without so much as a courtesy knock, two men in familiar black suits ventured into the room, their gazes fixated on Gideon. Gideon wondered if they were part of the group that brought in Leroux. He frankly couldn't tell any of them apart. But Healer Airmid swooped in front of the men, her face reminding Gideon of a thundercloud, halting their progress into the room.

"See, he's awake," one of the men sneered at Airmid. The man was taller and older than his dark-haired companion.

"His body has been through unbelievable trauma. Even with the accelerated healing we are doing, he's going to have to stay in this hospital for at least a week. And even I won't be able to erase all the scarring. Your questions can wait." Gideon thought that Healer Airmid looked like she was vibrating she was so pissed.

"You can answer just a few questions, can't you?" the agent said to Gideon, saying the words like they were a challenge.

"Sure," Gideon responded. He would rather get it over with and not have to have these guys come back later.

Healer Airmid huffed in aggravation, but her shoulders dropped in defeat when she glanced at Gideon. "My word is law here. If I say he needs a break or to rest, you will not question me. I will happily have you escorted from the premises and permanently banned if you don't follow my command. Do you understand?"

The men both looked properly cowed by the diminutive healer. The second man, who hadn't said anything previously, turned and gave Gideon a patently fake smile. "We are aware that you are recovering, and we hate to bother you while you're healing, but it is very important that we find out what happened. We need to ensure no one else ends up going through what you did. We'd just like to ask a few questions and if at any time you need a break, you just tell us, okay?"

"You don't have to answer these men's questions," Gideon's mom snarled. "They can come back later. My son saved our lives, and he has earned some rest."

"It's okay, Ma. I can answer a couple of questions."

The two agents glanced at one another. Gideon got the sense that they were able to communicate with just a look. The older of the two, a man with a sharp and hawkish countenance, addressed

Gideon's mother. "Mrs. Bean," he began, his voice a deep rumble at odds with his narrow face. "Some of what we have to discuss with Gideon and Miss Menet is sensitive information. It's classified."

Stella Bean, a woman of formidable resolve, frowned at the pair of agents. She threw a protective glance at Gideon. "Classified?" she retorted, an iron edge to her words. "This is my own son we're talking about. I've a right to know what is going on."

Gideon saw the determined gleam in his mother's eyes. "It's okay, Ma," he reassured her, offering a small, strained smile. "Could you go grab me a soda and some chips from the cafeteria? I'll catch you up when we're done here, promise."

His mom continued to ignore the agents, keeping her eyes trained on her son. Reluctantly, she agreed, but not without a handful of pointed looks at the interlopers. As the door closed behind his mother, Gideon turned his attention back to the Conclave agents.

Studying the duo further, Gideon could feel his senses prickling. The younger and somewhat nicer agent, carried the faint hint of a magical aura. It reminded him of Mrs. Sousa – the woman who'd been a wolf shifter. Gideon concluded that the quiet agent was most likely something similar.

Shaking his head as if to clear it, Gideon turned his attention to the other agent. The man gave off a feeling of smug superiority, his eyes scanning the room, over the heads of the room's occupants as if they were below his notice. Gideon pushed his awareness towards the man, trying to make sense of the swirling energy he felt pulsing from him. Unexpectedly prominent were the sensations of blood and hunger.

A creeping unease began to slither into Gideon's gut. The sanguine craving and barely leashed predatory instinct he felt coming off the man didn't sit well. It was unfamiliar and yet, somehow, instinctively recognizable, like a primordial memory was pricking his brain that he couldn't fully recall.

"Nervous, Mr. Bean?" The agent's voice was silken, sardonic. It took Gideon a moment to realize he was the focus of the sharp question. He blinked in response, silent.

The agent's keen eyes tracked his unease. Gideon swallowed hard, keeping his gaze locked on the man despite the thick, pressing wave of discomfort that made his skin goosebump.

The clarity of the blood-hunger sensation pulsating was unnerving. It was such a strong sensation, it made Gideon want to escape the room. Doubt and confusion warred within him as he tried to reconcile the sensation with the agent standing wordlessly before him.

"Are you a vampire?" Gideon blurted out.

The agent jolted as if shocked but quickly recovered giving Gideon a weirdly pleased smile. Gideon was suddenly and uncomfortably aware of the man's teeth. Were the agent's canines longer than they should be, or was Gideon seeing things?

The second agent stepped closer, pulling Gideon's attention away from the other man's teeth. "He is. What do you think I am?"

"Um… you remind me of this shifter woman I met. She was a wolf, but… I don't think you're that. I *am* picking up on something predatory with… fur? Maybe something feline?"

"Nice. I'm a tiger shifter." The man turned back to the other agent with a wide smile before turning to Dacey. "You said he's untrained, yeah? That's impressive as hell then. I'd like to talk to you more about your abilities, but first, we really do need to talk to you about what happened this morning. Can we sit?"

When Gideon reluctantly nodded, the two men pulled over chairs, seating themselves opposite his bed from Dacey. The healer took a position near the door, looking like she was ready to toss them out at the slightest sign from Gideon. One of them retrieved a recording device and placed it on the table.

Gideon stared at the recorder for a long moment, a weird sense of apprehension filling him. He didn't really want to talk about what happened in those woods. It was all so horrible and still so fresh that he wanted some time to process it. Talking about it made it real.

His story was also going to be pretty damn gruesome, and he didn't think Dacey needed to be traumatized by finding out that he had thrown himself into a campfire on purpose.

However, wanting things didn't make them happen and he knew he was just delaying the inevitable. So, Gideon recounted the events, his voice surprisingly steady as he relayed what had transpired after they'd been knocked unconscious at his apartment. He tried to make sure he recalled every detail, ensuring nothing was omitted.

"I'm not sure why I woke up before everyone else," Gideon said.

The agent who seemed nicer than the other explained, "It's probably due to you being an auramancer. You are often less affected by magic and potions than other people."

"Huh," was all Gideon could muster in response.

He took a small breath, his voice steady as he continued recounting the events that unfolded after he awoke. As he reached the part where he rolled both Dacey and himself into the scorching fire, a shocked sound escaped from the bennu shifter. His gaze flickered towards Dacey, his heart wrenching at the sight of horror and shock painted across her face. He desperately wanted to shield her from this part of the story. He hesitated for a moment, until the nice agent discreetly cleared his throat, encouraging him to continue. Once Gideon finished describing the aftermath of the explosion, he tried to explain how he sensed the poltergeist nearby.

"That wasn't a poltergeist," the vampire agent interrupted. "That was an incorporeal Deimos demon."

Gideon turned towards Dacey, repeating in disbelief, "A demon? Like from hell? And it was trying to possess humans like in *The Exorcist?*"

Dacey shook her head. "Not really. Deimos demons aren't quite like the demons you're thinking of. For one thing, they don't have anything to do with the hell depicted in Christianity, although they are superficially similar. They originate from the Infernal realm, which is similar in some ways to hell, with the heat and fire and such, but there is no Satan as far as we know. And human souls aren't banished there as punishment after death."

"Realm?" Gideon repeated slowly, like he was testing out the word.

Dacey's brow furrowed as she tried to clarify. "There are people who could explain this better than me but... Okay, so, we're here on Earth, but there are lots of other worlds in other dimensions. The Infernal realm is one of those dimensions. We can access some of these other realms, and they can access us through special magical portals. Each realm has its own distinct dangers and peculiarities. And often, its own species. For example, Valkyries come from the Valhalla realm, and the Fae come from the Fae realm. Some portals have been sealed shut permanently due to the realms' hazardous atmospheres or the dangers their inhabitants present, like Mount Olympus. Earth is the nexus, or... I like to think of us like Grand Central Station. We're the main hub – they all connect through this realm."

The shifter Conclave agent picked up what Dacey was explaining, "Of all the realms, Earth holds a pivotal role. We are a vital hub, intricately connected to these other dimensions. It is immensely important to protect Earth and its citizens from the danger these realms can occasionally pose. We also must protect our people from themselves, from their own discrimination against Mythical beings. If humans knew about the other realms, they'd probably campaign to close all portals. Which, for one thing, is impossible, and, for another, some of our scientists have theorized that it could cause our environment to destabilize.

However, over the centuries, we have closed a few portals, like the one to the Infernal realm."

The vampire agent jumped in next. "The Deimos are a menacing demon-like species. However, in their natural state, they are ethereal and insubstantial, which is how they are able to survive in their realm. They like to come into our realm and use magic to possess people – they *love* having physical bodies. But they're violent, dangerous sadists. So, we've closed every portal they've ever tried to open."

Dacey continued, "Every time we close one portal to the Infernal realm, the Deimos almost immediately get to work trying to open a new one. These demons apparently had found a spot in the Blackwater River State Forest, where the veil between their realm and ours was thin, so that's where they were trying to open a portal using sacrificial blood magic. It was in the middle of a protected forest, so they might've gotten away with it if it hadn't been for you. I swear, the Deimos love the South. My theory is they like the heat. Reminds them of home."

Gideon's heart filled with worry as he turned to the agent. "Do you think there might be more of the demons still out there?" His mind kept replaying the moment when Kaminski had cut Dacey's throat.

The shifter agent's face tightened with hesitation as he considered Gideon's question. "We don't believe so," he finally replied, trying to offer reassurance. "However, we have called in a psychic who specializes in sensing demons. She's going to be combing this entire region to ensure that no demons have escaped."

Agent Vampire-Jerk quickly added, "That is nothing for you to worry about, Mr. Bean. Right now, we just need you to finish telling us what happened next. How did you know you could grab the incorporeal Deimos?"

Gideon didn't appreciate this guy's suspicious expression. "I didn't know that I could, actually. I reacted without thought. All I knew was that I was desperate for it not to escape, so I lunged at it instinctively."

The agent didn't look convinced, but Gideon didn't give a shit. He continued with the rest of the tale.

Gideon's voice was shaky yet filled with determination as he asked the question foremost in his mind: "So... Kaminski, Leroux, and that golf guy were possessed by demons. Were the humans inside them aware of what the demons were doing?"

The shifter agent cleared his throat before replying. "They're not conscious or aware, thankfully. When the Deimos takes over, it's like the human inside the body is asleep. When it leaves, they just wake up with no memory of what happened."

Gideon's heart pounded against his ribs. An icy chill ran down his spine. "Is it possible that the demons abandoned their hosts when Dacey killed them? Could they have escaped? I didn't sense any spirits afterward, except the one that had been inside Leroux."

The vampire agent shook his head. "No, when Dacey grabbed them, her fire trapped them inside their hosts as she burned them out."

"Does that mean Dacey... that she killed two innocent humans when she burned out the demons?" Gideon cut his eyes toward Dacey, feeling like a jerk for bringing it up. Her gaze stared fixedly at her hands that were clasped together between her knees. Her brow was scrunched up like Gideon's words had wounded her.

The silence seemed to expand, filling every crevice of the room before the agent replied with a certain heaviness in his voice, "Yes. But Miss Menet couldn't have known what she was dealing with. As far as she was aware, she was killing two men in self-defense."

Aggravated with himself over his thoughtless questions, Gideon said, "Yeah, she saved our lives. I'd be dead if it wasn't for Dacey."

Dacey's head popped up and when her eyes met Gideon's, he gave her a grateful smile.

After that, the agents continued to ask the same questions repeatedly, just changing the wording. Gideon's body began to betray him as exhaustion started to swamp him. His vision blurred, and his eyelids grew heavy as weariness washed over him. The healer stepped forward and declared to the agents, "You gentlemen have two minutes to finish asking your questions, and then you have to leave."

"Gideon," Agent Vampire-Jerk asked, "can you describe what the Deimos' magic felt like to you?"

Gideon took a deep breath. "Their magic… it was dark and heavy. It almost felt like suffocating. It was black, burning heat that made me feel nauseous. Like coils of poisonous dark vapor. It was malevolent, twisted, and corrupted. It felt like a sticky, foul darkness on my skin –like evil and death."

Healer Airmid announced that the agents' time was up and that they could come back tomorrow if they had more questions.

The nicer agent shook his head, pulling a business card out of his pocket. "I don't think that will be necessary. I believe we got everything we needed. However, Mr. Bean, if you think of anything else, please call us."

With respectful nods, the two men exited the room, and soon Gideon fell asleep.

CHAPTER 28

*D*acey's voice was the first thing Gideon heard when he next woke up. He opened his eyes and glanced around the darkened hospital room. He wasn't sure, but it felt like early morning to him. His mom was asleep in a cot not far away, but he didn't see Dacey. Her voice was coming from just outside his room.

He could see her pacing just outside his door, a phone pressed to her ear. Gideon was about to try to get back to sleep when he heard her say his name. His ears immediately perked right back up.

"You need to understand. Gideon pulled an incorporeal Deimos demon out of thin air and was able to hold on to it. Not only that, he gave it enough substance that I was able to burn it out of existence. With that kind of power, the other Conclaves are going to be salivating over him, I'm just saying. He hasn't even had proper training. If you let him get sniped by someone else, you're going to be kicking yourself for years. You need to make an offer and it better be a good one."

Dacey continued to pace back and forth before her footsteps carried her away from Gideon's door. Her voice faded and

Gideon strained his ears to catch what else she had to say, but all he could hear was quiet murmuring. Soon enough, she reappeared in his doorway, a satisfied expression gracing her features as she ended her phone call. Catching the sight of Gideon awake, she broke into a cheerful smile.

Before he could inquire about her phone call, Healer Airmid arrived and made her way into the room.

"Good morning, Gideon. I hope you slept well. If you're up for it, I'd like to do some more healing on your burns before breakfast."

Gideon nodded. The sooner she healed him, the sooner he could go home.

"Hey, Gid. How are you feeling?" Dacey asked quietly, taking the chair next to his bed.

Gideon shrugged. "Pretty good surprisingly."

Healer Airmid came over and placed a soft hand on his forehead. Gideon could feel her magic wash through his body like a soft cool wave. She hummed lowly, her forehead wrinkled with concentration. Removing her hand, she opened her eyes and gave him a pleased smile.

"You're making good progress. How does your shoulder feel?"

Gideon reached up and prodded his sore collarbone. "It aches a little, but it's not that bad."

She nodded. "It should finish healing on its own now. Just don't lift anything heavy or do any strenuous exercise for the next few weeks."

When Gideon agreed to take it easy, she turned to prep for his burn treatment. He watched as the healer puttered around the room, gathering supplies.

The noise must've woken his mom as she rolled over and sat up. She gave a jaw-cracking yawn, looking blearily around the room. The confusion cleared from her face when she spotted Gideon in his hospital bed. She scrambled off her cot, her hair in a wild tangle. "How are you feeling?"

"I'm good, Ma. The healer – I mean doctor – is going to work on my burns." Gideon looked at his mom's tired face and felt guilty. "Why don't you head home and get some rest? Seriously, I'm fine now, and this place is only a couple of hours from home. Or what about the hotel that Dacey's company has offered you? It's free and you could get some rest."

His mom huffed. "No way. Dr. Airmid got me permission to stay by your side for as long as you're here."

"Uh, what about your job? I don't want you to get fired."

"I told Mr. Donovan that I was going to be in the hospital with you until you got discharged – no matter what. He tried to kick up a fuss, but I told him I would quit, and he'd be on his own. You got attacked by two serial killers – how can he possibly expect me to come to work at a time like this! Someone from the company Dacey works for – that Nexus Consulting company – called and explained to me how to apply for a medical leave of absence so we don't have to worry about lost wages. I guess they were thankful for your help in solving the case. I still can't believe that you and Dacey were chasing murderers. If you ever do something so stupid ever again, I swear to all that is holy…"

Gideon thought about the phone call he'd overheard. If the Conclave was willing to help his mom like that, when it didn't really benefit them… If they really made him a job offer, he would seriously consider it. Having an employer willing to go to bat for their employees would be a new and novel experience for Gideon.

Healer Airmid rolled over a small table covered in supplies. Taking a seat next to his bed, she gave him an expectant look. "Are you ready to get started?"

"I guess."

The healer turned to his mom with a smile. "Mrs. Bean, do you think you could go out and let the nursing station know that Gideon is up? He'll need to have breakfast delivered when I'm done dressing his wounds. Good nourishment is vital to recovery."

Gideon's mother hovered in the doorway, her face pinched with concern. Her eyes flickered from her son's thickly bandaged arms to the healer who stood by his bedside. "Gideon," she said, pulling her gaze away from Healer Airmid, "do you have any requests for breakfast?"

Gideon twisted his lips into a semblance of a smile. The pain medication had left him fuzzy-headed, but he sought to reassure her. "You can pick whatever, Ma. You know what I like."

That seemed to comfort her, as she nodded, her fingers clenching and unclenching around the door handle. "Can I grab anything for you, Dacey?" his mom offered.

Dacey shook her head. "I already ate, but thank you, Stella."

Then his mom turned around and hustled out of the room, calling out over her shoulder a promise to return soon. His mother's presence and absence filled the room like a tide, coming in gentle pushes only to recede just as quickly into silence.

The serene quiet was briefly broken as Gideon turned to the healer. "I don't want her to see you… you know, doing all that magic stuff. She wouldn't understand any of it. I don't want to worry her, and I definitely don't want one of you guys trying to erase her memories."

Healer Airmid did not bat an eye but smiled in a knowing way. The slight crinkles around her eyes softened her face, giving her an air of serenity as she placed a comforting hand on Gideon's shoulder. "Don't worry, Gideon," she soothed. "The nurses will keep your mother busy until we're done with the treatment." Her words carried the authority of one well-acquainted with the running of the healing ward, a master of her domain, promising safety not only from his physical maladies but also from the potential turmoil his supernatural ordeal could cause.

"Okay, let's get this done. What are you going to do?"

"I'm going to put this healing salve on your burns and then use my magic to encourage your body to heal. Your body is somewhat resistant to my magic so this will be slower and more uncomfortable to you than most Mythicals. Are you alright to get started?"

When Gideon nodded, she began to carefully unwind the bandages encasing his arms. Expecting to see charred flesh or red angry blisters, he was stunned to find that his skin was instead weirdly smooth and a dark pink hue. The absence of arm hair made his skin look fake, like he was an android or something.

He held his arm up, rotating it to look at it from all angles. "Weird."

Healer Airmid looked up from where she was uncapping a tube. "What?"

"I look like a naked mole rat."

His complaint made Dacey and Airmid sputter out a chuckle.

"I've never heard that description before. It's just new skin. Between the burn lotion," Airmid held up a small tube, "and my magic, I was able to get your body to grow new skin."

Squirting a large amount of a pale yellow cream onto one hand, the healer gave Gideon a warning. "This is going to be uncomfortable, just to warn you. You were unconscious for the worst of it yesterday, but it's still going to be unpleasant. The important thing is to not scratch your new skin. And, I promise, you're gonna want to. I'm going to need you to relax as much as possible. When I push my magic into you, I want you to concentrate on accepting it."

"Great," Gideon said, laying the sarcasm on syrupy thick.

When the healer started to smear the lotion onto one of Gideon's arms while quietly murmuring incantations in a foreign language, it felt cool and soothing at first. But soon his skin started to tingle. That irritating sensation gradually morphed into a burning itch. Determined to resist scratching, he clenched his teeth, resolved not to disrupt the healing process. It felt like searing heat prickling up and down his arms. His fingers started twitching without any signal from his brain and he kept shifting restlessly on his bed.

"How long does this last?" Gideon asked through clenched teeth, the itching making him start to feel insane.

"About twenty minutes."

Gideon started cussing under his breath. "Why not just knock me out?"

"Your magic is resistant to mine, so it works better with you actively working with me. I could knock you out, but you'd have to stay here much longer."

Once done with his arms, the healer had Gideon remove his shirt so she could work on his back. "This is going to hurt worse."

When Gideon made a wordless sound of complaint, Healer Airmid clucked her tongue in reprimand. "Your back took the brunt of the burns. Turns out that pouring the contents from a boiling cauldron on your back is a bad idea."

"Okay, fine. Let's do this."

Airmid smeared the lotion on his back and started chanting. Immediately Gideon's back felt like a swarm of fire ants were biting him. He'd once fallen into a patch of stinging nettles, and somehow, this sensation was worse than that.

"Aw shit, this sucks. Someone distract me," he commanded when the burning and itching started to become unbearable. "Dacey, what happened with Leroux?"

"From what Santos told me, Quinn questioned him, and he didn't remember anything. He had no recollections of the last four weeks. His last memory was playing golf at Eglin. Quinn interviewed him for more than an hour. At first, they thought maybe he was managing to lie, that he was resistant to her magic. Then they were worried that we'd somehow made a mistake and arrested the wrong guy. Santos said that he was completely bewildered, and he thought he was having a nervous breakdown. They wanted you to come back and test Leroux for magic. When you didn't answer your phone and then I didn't answer mine, they realized something was very wrong. Wiz was at my hotel room, grabbing something personal of mine to do a location spell when my emergency call came through after we killed the demons, and you passed out."

"How did your phone survive?" Gideon asked, thinking of how all her clothes had been burnt to ash.

"It didn't, actually. We were lucky. Your mom had her phone on her."

Gideon was shaking and gritting his teeth as Airmid kept working on his back. He couldn't stop twitching. "What is going to happen to Mr. Peterson?"

"Oh, he's going to jail. Once Leonhard went through his financial records, it was easy to find plenty of evidence of embezzlement and fraud."

"So, he really didn't know about the demons?"

"He had no clue. He was just a greedy asshole who got caught with his pants down and they were able to blackmail him."

By the time the itching finally settled down, Gideon was so exhausted that he could barely keep his eyes open through breakfast. Once he finished his rubbery eggs and toast, he was losing the battle to stay awake.

Dacey sat on his bedside and gave him an unhappy look. "Hey, I'm sorry to have to tell you this but I need to go. I have to let all the parents know what really happened to their kids and I don't think a phone call is enough. I need to look each of them in the eye and tell them what happened to their children. And once I'm done with that, the Conclave is sending me on another assignment. I'm not sure how long it's going to be, but I'll try to come back and visit you here if I can."

That woke Gideon right back up. "Wait. You have to go right now?"

"Yeah, they think a gremlin nest has infested the Atlanta

airport and is causing malfunctions. It can get dangerous because those guys love to feed on electronics."

Gideon tried to hide his disappointment. He'd somehow built up a fantasy in his head that they'd start working together as a team. "Are gremlins dangerous?" Gideon asked.

"Not really." Dacey glanced at her watch and growled. "Shit. I need to go now if I'm going to visit all the parents. I've got your number, Giddy. I'll text, okay?"

"Sounds good. Stay safe, Candy!"

"Ha ha," Dacey griped. She gave him one long look, then turned on her heels and exited.

Gideon stared at the door for a very long time.

EPILOGUE

"Hey, Giddy! I got a new one for you. I don't think you've ever met one of these!"

Gideon turned to his co-worker Silas who was pushing a gurney topped with a large cardboard box.

"Oh yeah?"

"Yeah, this guy is super rare. I'm excited to see what you feel!"

Silas removed the top from the box. He looked on eagerly as Gideon stared at the cloth-covered body inside. From the shape and size, all Gideon could tell was that it was probably a man. Pulling one of his thick gloves off, he hovered his hand over the corpse and released his magic. The fluorescent lights overhead caught on the thin spidery scars crawling down Gideon's forearm. The scars looked like delicate, jagged lightning bolts that were almost silvery. Thankfully, his arm hair had finally grown back in, and the scars were hardly noticeable unless you were looking for them. Healer Airmid had done an amazing job trying to erase the evidence of his romp in the fire.

"Feels like some sort of animal. Pretty strong magic. I'm getting feathers, I think. So, some type of bird." Gideon tilted his head and pushed on his magic. "Wait, not just feathers. I'd swear I'm also sensing fur. And – something like that basilisk we got last week? But it's not snake-like, if that makes sense – I'm not picking up any scales. The venom, maybe."

Gideon opened his eyes and stared down at the mummified-looking corpse. "A hippogriff? I think I was reading about them the other day."

Silas gave him a good-natured nudge, and the satyr's magic brushed against Gideon's senses. "You're close, but no cigar. This guy was a manticore."

Gideon gave Silas a blank look, having never heard of that type of Mythical. Silas gave him another grin, his eyes bright and pleased having stumped Gideon. "A manticore has a human head with the body of a lion. It has wings and a tail with venomous spikes."

"Huh," was all Gideon could think to say. He put the lid back on the box and helped Silas slide the manticore into the retort.

Gideon pulled the small notebook that he kept in his back pocket and made an entry for the manticore. He was keeping the journal at Vena's suggestion. She sent him a book of her own notes of her descriptions of magic so he could compare what his senses picked up against another auramancer's. It had been an invaluable tool for understanding and recognizing all types of magic.

Vena also sent him a weekly 'care package' filled with Mythical artifacts to familiarize himself with all varieties of magic. She'd even flown down twice in the month since he'd been released from the hospital to work with him in person. The Savannah Conclave funded all his training. The Conclave representative had fallen all over herself to get Gideon to sign a contract. Santos, who had visited him in the hospital several times and had turned out to be a great friend, had suggested to Gideon that he had enormous negotiating power. With Santos's mentoring, Gideon had gotten the Mythical agency to get him a new job at the Conclave-owned Tranquil Haven crematorium at a salary that made Gideon grin every time he thought about it, plus free training, paid travel expenses, and tons more perks. They'd even agreed to sponsor him going back to college in the fall. He'd had to sign a non-compete contract, but he'd decided it was easily worth it.

They'd even paid him a nice, hefty fee for helping take out the Deimos demons.

Once he set the timer on the oven, Gideon straightened suddenly, familiar magic washing over his senses only a moment before his ears detected an easily recognizable voice. It was a voice he thought about more often than he cared to admit.

"I had the guy totally cornered with his pants down. Literally. Found him in a bathroom stall at a rest stop right off I-75."

The door swung open and there Dacey was dressed like a preschool teacher in khaki pants, a flowery blouse covered in a pink cardigan, with a phone pressed to her ear. When she spotted Gideon, she gave him a wide happy grin. "I've got to go. I'll send in my report later tonight," Dacey said to whoever was on the other end of the line.

Hanging up the phone, she skipped over to him and threw herself into Gideon's arms. "Giddy! I've missed you. Talking to you on the phone just isn't cutting it."

"I've missed you too. It's been, what – a month? Why are you dressed like an elementary school librarian?"

Dacey pulled back and made a face. "Ugh. I was on assignment. Needed to blend in."

Gideon decided to save his plethora of questions about the assignment later. He had a more important question to ask: "What are you doing here?"

She gave him a bright, mischievous smile that he'd missed so much it made his lungs ache. "I've got a case and I could use your help… It's gonna be fun."

. . .

To Be Continued...

ACKNOWLEDGMENTS

Thank you so much for reading my book! I hope you are as glad to be back in the world of Mythicals as I am. This series is set in the same world as Sophie Feegle not long after the time frame of Sophie and The Odd Ones. You'll notice a reference in the book to the druid sacrifices in Cascadia, an event that happened in book 3.

I need to thank my family for all of their support. Thanks to my beta readers: David, Jessica, Jillian, Joanne, Karen, Leon, Paige, Pam, Rachel, and Susan. I'd like to thank my book cover artist Rebecacovers, and my editor Arundhati Subhedar.

If you enjoyed *Gideon Bean*, please leave a review – it really helps indie writers like me.

ABOUT THE AUTHOR

Gwen DeMarco is an avid reader, wine & coffee drinker, gardener and a lover of all things nerdy. Gwen loves to write paranormal romance novels with a focus on the weird and wonderful. She loves to write a good snarky heroine and a grumpy male lead. Sophie Feegle is her first foray into the world of shifters, fae, ogres and vampires.

Gwen is happily married to her high school sweetheart and has two teenage children. She can often be found with her nose in a book and a glass of wine or mug of coffee in her hand.

Sign up to her mailing list and receive a **free** copy of a novella of Mac's point of view from meeting Sophie from Sophie and The Odd Ones.

To learn more, please visit my website and sign up for my mailing list to receive updates at www.GwenDeMarco.com

ALSO BY GWEN DEMARCO

Sophie Feegle Series

Sophie and The Odd Ones

Portents and Oddities

Odd Times for Sophie Feegle

Against All Odds

Odds and Ends

Kingdom of Erishum Trilogy

The Mudlark

The Gutter Shrike

The Dying Wilds

Auras & Embers

Gideon Bean